Beautiful Girl

ELISABETH OGILVIE

SCHOLASTIC BOOK SERVICES
New York Toronto London Auckland Sydney Tokyo

Cover Photo by Owen Brown

ISBN 0-590-31277-4

Copyright © 1980 by Elisabeth Ogilvie. All rights re-
served. Published by Scholastic Book Services, a division
of Scholastic Magazines, Inc.

14 13 12 11 10 9 8 7 6 5   1 2 3 4 5/8

Printed in the U. S. A.   06

Beautiful Girl

A Wildfire Book

One

The first two long words I remember saying were "adorable" and "persnickety." In one memorable day I used them both for the first time.

I was just four and had spent an enchanting day with my three Snow cousins who lived in the country and had a brook running through their field. Brendan, the oldest, was eight, and I thought he was wonderful. I'd have fetched and carried for him until I dropped. "Persnickety" was a new word he had begun to use on his sisters when they rebelled against his orders. It had a good, crisp, lively sound; I practiced it silently to myself while we labored on his miniature village and harbor on the bank of the brook.

In mid-afternoon, Aunt Margaret called us up to the house for milk and cookies. Some ladies were having tea with her on the porch.

"And who is this *adorable* little girl?" one of them asked. I knew well the tone and the expression. Sometimes I think I was born knowing it, and I'd heard the word many times too. But today, suddenly, it became mine. Like "persnickety."

"She's our stupid cousin," Brendan volunteered amiably.

They looked shocked, and Aunt Margaret said, *"Brendan."* She explained that I was Tom and Karen's daughter, and shooed us off the porch with our jug of milk, paper cups, and box of cookies.

"Go back to the brook and have a nice picnic," she said. The cooing followed us. For all I cared it could have been the morning talk of the pigeons under the eaves at home, and a lot less interesting, since I was personally acquainted with the pigeons.

"Karen was always pretty, but this child will be a beauty. . . . She'll be tall like her father, and oh, that coloring! . . . Just adorable!"

Aunt Margaret changed the subject. I was used to that too. "Adorable," I whispered as we trooped back to the brook. "Ah-do or-uh-bull." What a satisfying music it made. Almost as good as "persnickety."

In late afternoon my mother came to get me. I talked non-stop all the way home. I was still going strong by the time we reached the house, and there was Jones, our terrier-from-the-pound, waiting to play. We were milling noisily around when my father came home. My mother was calling me to wash my hands and set the table, but I kept Jones barking his head off so as to drown her out.

My tall father walked in on this uproar, which ceased abruptly. I rushed to him for the usual embrace, and he said, "How's my future law partner?"

I leaned back from his shoulder and said, "I'm adorable."

"Oh? Who says so?"

"Everybody!"

"Well, I don't know how adorable you are right now," he said. "I do know your mother wants you to set the table and you aren't doing it, and I know you're pretty dirty too. So you'd better get busy." He put me down and started me toward the kitchen.

"Don't be persnickety," I said pertly.

To this day that word means two sharp slaps and a stinging sensation on the bottom.

I never used it again to either parent, and I learned a lot more words and when to use or not to use them. I also learned that my parents didn't want to hear me telling them that I was adorable, beautiful, lovely, breathtaking, or any of those other things I kept hearing about myself.

When I was about six my mother told me that they loved me because I was their child, and it had nothing to do with my being pretty or plain. This is when I first heard that Handsome is as Handsome does.

And of course there was always Brendan, who felt it was his duty to keep his sisters and me from getting above ourselves. No problem here, since I worshipped him.

I liked school, the sociability of it and the adventure of learning something new all the time, whether it was a lovely word or a game or a song. Life was rich and varied, with a lot of fun even in spite of the occasional reminders that Handsome is as Handsome does, and the times when I sat in my room with orders to *think* about what I'd just done or hadn't done. Or had my feelings hurt in the schoolyard and burst into tears, and thought too late of a killing answer.

However, I always bounced back quickly from these things. As far as I was concerned I was an ordinary, happy-go-lucky kid.

Then came the new girl in the third grade, and the end of my special kind of innocence, when I realized for the first time that my looks were a handicap.

TWO

Phyllis Clements had just moved into town, and because she came from Cleveland, Ohio, (what a magical, poetic pair of words in those days!) we thought she was terribly sophisticated. She had yellow hair in bangs, bright blue eyes, a square chin, an impudent nose that belonged with the way she walked and the way she could give her simplest statement an authority we wouldn't dare to dispute.

The rest of us were slightly in awe of Miss Trimble, who was new this year and therefore an unknown quantity. But Phyllis had known teachers practically the world around; after all, she came from Cleveland, Ohio. She seemed to find Miss Trimble a pretty mediocre specimen. Not that she was ever rude. She didn't have to be. Her air of careless power said it all.

She was a demon at schoolyard sports. When she couldn't muscle in on the boys' games, she brought a soccer ball and introduced the game to her special choices among the girls. When she wasn't rushing across the playground like a comet with a tail of followers, she was surrounded by them in a corner, relating the hair-raising events that went on in the big schools where she'd been.

I wanted passionately to be one of her chosen audience. In my secret soul, where lived a longing for a Best Friend, I dreamed of finding one, and Phyllis Clements had suddenly become It.

One morning at recess I'd gone in to get a drink, and when I came back to the open doors, Miss Trimble and Mrs. Munro were standing outside in the sun. I was about to go by when I heard my name, and stopped behind them.

"April Adams is the most beautiful child I've ever seen," Miss Trimble said. "I have a hard time keeping my eyes off her."

"And she's completely unspoiled so far," said Mrs. Munro. "Which is the way we want to keep it. She's a nice youngster, and there's a pretty good brain under that golden hair and behind those sea-green eyes."

"With eyes like that, who needs a brain?" Then Miss Trimble laughed. "I'm sure she'll be hearing that a few hundred times in her future."

"Yes, poor kid," said Mrs. Munro. I didn't wait to hear more. I skidded out when they were investigating a wrangle. I was intent on joining Phyllis's circle. At least I could get into the outer rim, which would make me look like one of the gang.

I wasn't elated by what I'd just overheard. I'd been hearing it for most of my eight years, in spite of my relatives' efforts, so all I thought now was something like, "Oh, more of that old stuff."

However, there were favors to be got from Miss Trimble, like being chosen often to tidy the bookshelves or water the plants, or to re-arrange the stuff that came to rest on the grand piano. This had been a gift to the school from the richest people in town. Our room was the biggest, so we got the piano, and Miss Trimble could play it, which gave our class a certain prestige.

I hoped that being chosen to do these things would give me some importance in Phyllis's eyes.

In the fall the piano held a big vase of autumn flowers and, along the curving side nearest the blackboard, the apples-for-recess. Some of us prudently put our apples into our desks at once, but there were a few chronic offenders who kept dropping their fruit, or crunching on it, and these had to leave their apples on the piano, each in its own special place so there'd be no problems of identification. They were hidden from the class by the books, magazines, and flowers.

This is a significant matter in my life history.

Miss Trimble sent us up to the board two at a time to work out whatever multiplication tables we were weak in. I was feeble in the eights, while Phyllis had trouble with the nines. (The only weakness I'd yet seen in her.) The day we were sent together to the board was like the day when I received my first big doll carriage — a complete surprise, and it wasn't even Christmas or my birthday.

I smiled at Phyllis when we reached the board, but her look was calm and cold. When she promptly moved way in behind the piano, I didn't have the nerve to follow and be snubbed, even silently. But I stood as close as I could.

Phyllis was already at work. I went to war on the eights, pondering, figuring, erasing. It was a desperate battle through seven, eight, and nine, until I reached the blessed simplicity of ten and eleven.

I finished my table at last, and looked over to see how Phyllis was doing. She was through, and watching *me*.

And — Oh Day of Days! — she winked at me.

It was the first sign that she knew I existed. And that wink was so easy, so practiced. I'd have winked back but I knew my technique couldn't compare with hers.

At that moment Mrs. Munro came in with a new boy. While she talked with Miss Trimble, and the whole room was staring without mercy at the humble newcomer, Phyllis picked one of the apples off the piano, and took a bite out of it. She replaced it, took another apple and another bite, and so on along the row. She must have swallowed the bites practically whole. I watched in fascinated horror. She showed no expression at all except for that wink.

Now Miss Trimble was introducing the new boy and assigning him his seat. Phyllis had bitten hunks out of eight apples. We went back to our seats, Phyllis as calmly arrogant as ever, myself with my upper lip pulled down very long to keep my face straight. She'd winked at me; I'd watched; we were *friends*.

Miss Trimble checked our work, pronounced it good, and sent two more to the board. They didn't go near the piano, so they didn't see the apples. Nobody did until the recess bell rang and the owners converged on the piano.

Instant chaos. I sat there scarlet and trembling, wanting to hoot with uncontrolled laughter, while Phyllis tranquilly removed from her desk a small plastic bag of grapes.

Miss Trimble restored order with an unexpectedly powerful voice. Those whose apples hadn't been touched, or who had something in their desks for recess, were dismissed. I remember the new boy staring at us. He was small, dark, and solemn. The victims stood around, outraged, the evidence in their hands.

I was both frightened and excited, but Phyllis merely looked interested. She was wonderful.

"Now, Phyllis," Miss Trimble said, quite gently, "who did this?"

"Who did what?" asked Phyllis. Miss Trimble, still gentle, said, "You know very well *what*, and you know very well *who*. It was for pure mischief, I suppose. You might as well admit it."

All Phyllis's world-traveler's poise wasn't going to get her out of this, and I couldn't stand to see it. I went even redder and hotter, I gripped the sides of my desk, and Miss Trimble gave me a kind look and said, "I know it wasn't April."

That touched off something in me. "H-how do you know it wasn't me?"

"Because you wouldn't do such a thing."

"How do you know I wouldn't do such a thing?" After the first stammering rush, I was fine. How did she know? How did anyone know? How did *I* know? True, I hadn't thought of it, but if I *had* thought of it —

"As a matter of fact," I said, trying to sound like my father, "I did it. I always wanted to, so today I did it."

"April!" Miss Trimble was losing her composure. The others were all agog. They'd believe anything of Phyllis, but *April*? Who cried if anyone hurt her feelings?

"Anybody's innocent till they're proved guilty," I added, "and you can't prove Phyllis is guilty, because I am."

And then I looked triumphantly at Phyllis.

Her cheeks were apple-red, her jaw shoved forward. She was furious. "You're a liar!" she snapped at me. "*I* did it. You wouldn't have *dared*." Her contempt was dreadful. She stared at Miss Trimble. "What do you want

10

me to do? Stay after school? Bring in a bunch of apples tomorrow?"

"Everyone else go out," Miss Trimble said. "April, you go too."

"Miss Trimble, I did do it!" But it was weak. I was trying not to cry. I rushed to the girls' bathroom for shelter as well as for necessity, and there gave in to my noisy weeping, while outside in the schoolyard everybody screamed in heartless fun.

A fifth-grade girl came in, asked me if I was sick or had wet my pants. I shook my head, snuffling miserably, and she told me I'd better wash my face and forget about whatever it was. "You'll get over it," she said callously. I knew I never would.

On the surface everything was the same as usual for the rest of the morning, even Miss Trimble. But I knew that when we left at noon some of the kids would surround me and ask me why I'd said such a crazy thing. They'd look at me as if I'd suddenly turned into a freak. And then they'd say "We all knew it was Phyllis! *She'd* do things like that!"

I considered telling Miss Trimble that I felt sick and asking her to call my mother, but that would be lying and I'd already been a liar once today. No, I'd just have to outrun them or else put on a good stolid face and shrug and say, "You can't prove *she's* telling the truth, can you?"

But I'd never be able to do that. I was a

failure, and so young too. And so sorry for myself that the tears were hanging there ready to spill when Phyllis caught me outside the Elm Street gate. She and her group barred the pavement before me. The New Boy was standing there, watching with big dark eyes.

"*So!*" she said ferociously. "Who do you think you are, anyway, Little Miss Goody Two-shoes! Listen, you do your own thing and never mind taking credit for mine. You think you're a little princess around here! 'Oh, I'm so beautiful!' " she mimicked, floating her hands in the air. "And so *stuck-up!*" The other faces were ugly with laughter. "Listen, I'm *me* and *I* do what I want and it's *my* show, and nobody else's. Maybe everybody else thinks you're something special, but all you are is a stupid *doll* — and a bawl-baby," she added with some truth, because by now I had completely dissolved.

They all ran off laughing. I have a vague memory of the New Boy still lurking under a maple tree, and then I was running too, blindly, gulping and sobbing.

Three

Hiccuping, I tried to explain to my mother why I'd come home in such a state. Of course I left out the apples and the lie. I said incoherently that I couldn't be Phyllis's friend because she said I was stuck-up. She thought *I* thought I was a beautiful princess. "And I don't!" I howled. "I'm *not* stuck-up!"

"Of course you aren't," my mother consoled me. "Everybody else knows you aren't stuck-up, so what does one girl's opinion matter? She hardly even knows you."

How could I explain the wonderful dream in which Phyllis Clements from Cleveland, Ohio, became my Best Friend? My mother named off other girls. *They* all liked me, she said.

"How do you know?" I asked thickly. "Maybe they don't." I kept on sniffling, and hugging Jones, who resisted.

I hoped she'd be sorry enough for me to keep me home that afternoon. I could get into bed and read *The Borrowers* again, and be comforted with hot cocoa. Instead she drove me to school, getting me there just in time to go in. I took my seat without looking around, in case I should surprise a mean grin on anyone.

Phyllis had to replace all the apples she'd bitten, and stay after school. It didn't seem to bother her, and she was more admired than ever. But my life changed that day. Nothing was ever the same again. It had started with the apples, and I could well understand all the trouble Adam and Eve had gotten into.

I don't mean that I was miserable all the time, but now I was conscious of my appearance as never before, and gazed into my mirror a lot, wondering what made Phyllis so mad. I thought my mother was beautiful; she was tall, straight, and slender, with a long swift stride and a quick, lovely smile. But people were crazy to call *me* beautiful. My face was commonplace to me, just my face — like my feet. It was narrowing now, when it had once been round, but I still had my father's dimple in my left cheek. I was proud of *that*. Someone had called my eyes sea-green. I'd have rather had them dark blue with black lashes, like my cousins' eyes. My hair was blond to some, golden to others, and to me it was just hair that I hated having washed or brushed. I'd have preferred to have it cut off to look like Jones's coat instead of the long, sleek, Alice-in-Wonderland style my parents favored. Sometimes it was braided, and the braids looped up with ribbons. It was a nuisance, and I envied Jones. I'd gloried in my missing front teeth, and

14

without them I'd smiled at myself a lot in the mirror.

But even with the new teeth in straight, with no need of braces, it was just old *me* in the glass. Why should anyone think *I* thought I was special?

My parents must have gotten awfully tired of hearing Phyllis's name. "If you've always been nice to her," my mother said, "but she doesn't like you, that's her problem, not yours."

"She hates me, and she's the biggest problem of my whole life!"

"Only because you let her be," said my father. "You enjoyed life before Phyllis Clements ever came here. Now just ignore her and go on enjoying life. Let her stew in her own juice."

But how could I ignore her? If I wanted to, and worked at it, she wouldn't let me. I took care not to be ambushed again, never going near the Elm Street gate, but if I gave a good recitation, passed out papers, or was sent to deliver a message, I knew Phyllis would lie in wait after school to taunt me. I was getting used to "stuck-up" and its variations. But what the other kids said didn't matter. *I wanted Phyllis Clements to like me.*

Thanksgiving Day I told the whole story to Brendan, down by the brook after the big dinner. Claire, Kathleen, Jones, and their two Irish setters were with us. At least the girls were. Our dogs were racing round and round.

15

Brendan, twelve then, was very grown up and attentive. When I finished he said, "But you see, she did it to show off and you tried to steal her thunder."

"I just wanted to take the blame for her!"

"So she'd think you were great. Yeah, I know all about it. Well, she didn't think you were great, so forget it."

"*She* won't. She's always doing something dirty."

"She'll quit if she sees she can't make a dent in you. You go around asking to be kicked. She's a *jerk*, for Pete's sake! Just a plain, stupid, *jerk!*"

He sounded like my father, though with a different choice of words. But at least he understood the reason for the lie, so I could forget about that.

"Well, it's not very nice to think somebody hates you," Kathleen said. "Poor April."

"Why do you have to have everybody *like* you?" Brendan asked. "I know some guys who hate me! It's no skin off my nose. I couldn't care less."

"I can't help it," I said. "Nobody ever treated me like that before in my life, and I just wanted to be her friend. *I* don't think I'm a beautiful princess."

"But you do look like one," Claire told me judicially. "She's probably jealous. There's a girl in my room who's jealous of my naturally curly hair."

"Does she do mean things to you all the time?"

"She did till I twisted her arm around behind her when we were the only ones in the bathroom. You could do to that to Phyllis. Brendan'll show you how."

Brendan scowled. "April's got no killer instinct, and besides, this doozie probably knows karate already."

"I wish," I said despairingly, "that I had carrot-colored hair, bandy legs, and front teeth like a bunny rabbit's."

"Act the way she says you are," said Brendan. "Stuck-up. Float around like a princess. Like this." Since he was rangy and big-boned, his imitation had us rolling on the ground and in danger of falling into the brook.

Four

It was therapeutic. On Monday when I saw Phyllis in school there must have been something different about my expression, because it was Phyllis who looked away first. Later on she thought of a reason to go by my desk in art period and "accidentally" knocked over my water-color pan. Still fortified by Brendan, I didn't burst into tears, and I wasn't doing a very good picture anyway. But the hurt bewilderment was there, and it stayed. I had wanted Phyllis to like me, and she hated me.

In the fourth grade we were in separate rooms. She didn't have quite so many chances to mess up my desk-top, kick my ankle, and get behind me in line so as to give me a hard poke or a pinch. Outside I tried to stay away from her. I wasn't worried about physical hurt but of being mocked and tormented into those infuriating tears.

Even my usually understanding mother had a hard time understanding why I still wanted Phyllis Clements to like me. My father couldn't imagine why I even recognized her existence. I stopped mentioning her after he announced one night, "I would like to go through one meal without hearing You-Know-Who's name."

This year I started my career in dog-walking. I'd always taken Jones for walks, and because of a strict leash law I wasn't afraid of his being attacked by other dogs, or flinging a challenge at some wandering German shepherd who would instantly accept it. Mrs. Farrar next door asked me if I'd mind taking Heidi. She was a dachshund and good friends with Jones. He really enjoyed having somebody else along who was as interested in all the exciting smells. I got fifty cents a week, and never missed a walk unless it was raining.

Later another neighbor asked me to take his dog. Another fifty cents a week. Jock was an Airedale, and at first I took him alone; then I tried him with the two small dogs and the three got along fine. He just ignored Jones's challenges, so Jones decided to like him. Heidi looked up at him the way most of the girls gazed at Bobby Saxon, who was the fourth-grade boys' soccer champ. (Phyllis was the girls' champ, naturally.)

By summer I could be hired to give baths, and an elderly lady with arthritic hands paid me to groom her aging cocker spaniel and get the burrs out of his ears. I felt guilty about going away on vacation with my father and mother, but I still had my clients when I got back. The dogs loved me, and sometimes that seemed enough.

But things happened without warning.

Sharp stabs out of nowhere, taking your breath with the sheer surprise of them, putting tears in your eyes as if you'd suddenly cracked your shin or your crazy bone, or had a door slammed on your fingers.

I made a friend called Sharon, who danced partners with me at ballet recitals, dog-walked with me, spent recess with me, giggled a lot, and hated Phyllis as much as I did. She came to my tenth birthday party and we talked happily about hers — there'd be BOYS at it — and then suddenly she was avoiding me, looking furtive and guilty with no explanation whatever. And I wasn't invited to her party.

After the first shock of knowing that, I decided frantically to be sick on the day, so everybody would think that was why I wasn't there. But I didn't have to pretend. There was something going around, and I picked it up at the right time. When Sharon's birthday came on Friday, I was over the worst of it but lay in bed limp and dejected, wanting sympathy but not wanting Sharon's name mentioned.

I was ashamed too, as if I'd done something bad. I was worthless, a reject. I tried weeping into Jones's neck, but he wouldn't put up with it. He was more interested in all the delicious things my mother kept trying out on me. I didn't want them. All I could think of was the fabulous refreshments and the BOYS at Sharon's party, and how I was an outcast.

The hour of the party approached, and

somebody knocked at my door. It was Brendan, fourteen then, and looking as big as all outdoors in my small room. He smelled of the outdoors too, and looked heartlessly healthy. I rose up. "What are *you* doing here?"

Brendan never insulted me with lies. "My mother drove me in to keep you company while those stupid jerks are having their stupid party. Hey, aren't you starved by now?" he demanded. "I'm so hungry my stomach thinks my throat's cut. Aunt Karen says we can eat up here. Look, we stopped and got one of Galliano's Super-Giant Pizzas, with everything, and it's still hot."

"Okay," I said listlessly.

"And Uncle Tom's bringing home something good. If you weren't sick to begin with, you will be."

"I was *too* sick!" I sat up and glared at him. He dodged.

"Don't strike me!" he squealed. "I'm me mudder's only son!" He ducked out the door, then poked his face in. "And you look like Old Lady Witch's only daughter. You'd better brush your hair before you eat with me."

He ran downstairs, Jones barking delightedly at his heels. I stamped to the bathroom as hard as I could in bare feet, washed, and brushed my teeth. Back in my room I brushed my hair, making horrible grimaces at myself in the glass, and put on my quilted pale green robe with geranium-red ribbons, and plunked myself back into bed.

The next morning I woke up cheerful for the first time in days. Brendan and I took the dogs for an extra long walk to make up for three days' neglect. We went far out of town along the Cavendish Road, to a huge country estate where the people came only for July and August. It was spacious and serene, with a lovely view over the river and distant hills, and I made up my mind to come back again.

Then I went home with Brendan to the country for the weekend, by bus. My parents came out Sunday afternoon to get me. By late afternoon, when I was walking the dogs around streets scented with lilacs, I felt as if I could face anything.

But Monday morning the confidence was all gone. I must have shown the signs, because both parents had something to say. "Hold your head up," my mother said. "Don't let anyone think you cared that much. You had a lovely weekend and you'll have many more, besides a lot of other wonderful experiences in the years to come."

"When you put it all together," my father said, "not being invited to Sharon's party is just about as unimportant as anything can be." He kissed me and left. Of course it was unimportant to *him*, I thought gloomily.

"I wish that dumb old recital was over," I grumbled. "I won't dance with her."

"You can't let Miss Parris down."

"What about the stupid presents?" We'd picked them out with such pleasure, something from me and one from Jones too.

"Oh, you can give Sharon's to somebody else for Christmas, or take it to another birthday party."

"If I ever get invited," I said dismally.

"Then keep it for yourself. Go along now, you don't want to be late."

I did want to be late, I wanted to be absent forever. And there inside the fence, in the corner under the big maple where Sharon and I used to talk at recess, was Sharon and a knot of kids. Bobby Saxon was showing off by balancing his soccer ball on one finger, and Phyllis's bright head was close to Sharon's dark one. Phyllis's laughter was hearty.

Lightning struck in my stomach. So Phyllis *had* got Sharon!

Sharon and I danced through the recital without speaking. She and I had had great plans for this summer. They were dead now, but I still watered the grave with occasional tears. Every time I opened my top bureau drawer there were the presents, mine in violet-strewn paper with a bow to match, Jones's in a boyish pattern of sailboats. Mine was a pair of tiny Dutch shoes in blue and white china, on a fine chain. I didn't want to give them to anyone else, or to keep them. They were meant for Sharon's neck, and they haunted me.

Finally I wrote her a note. "Meet me this afternoon at the corner of your street and

Willow Drive. *If you don't come you'll be sorry.*"

Sharon sat at the back of our room, so in the morning confusion I made a trip around that way to the library shelves and managed to shove the note over her shoulder as I went by. She took it automatically.

I knew Sharon might not be there. She despised me now for Phyllis Clements's reasons, so why should she obey me? But if she wasn't there I'd go to her house and leave the presents on the doorstep, and shame her.

But there she was, sitting on the familiar stone wall where we used to meet, and Biscuit the poodle was beside herself with joy at meeting her friends again. Sharon looked stolid and sulky.

Oddly out of breath, I shoved the presents and cards at her. "One's from Jones. You might as well have them."

She didn't take them. Her face turned red, and her eyes filled. "Oh, April," she gasped. "I shouldn't."

"I bought them for you. What did Phyllis say about me?"

"Phyllis!" She gawked at me. "Nothing! It wasn't *her*. I had to ask her because my mother's acquainted with her mother."

"Then why didn't you ask me?" I could hardly believe I was saying it. "I asked you to mine. And I thought we were friends."

"We are! I had your invitation all addressed! But — "

24

"But what?" I had her on the witness stand, and I wouldn't let her go.

"My mother," she sniffled, getting even redder. "*She* said I shouldn't invite you . . . I should make some new friends because I'm getting older and it's important, because — "

"But why can't you keep your old friends?" I was relentless. "And still make new ones?"

"She says I don't need the competition."

"The *what*?" I put my hands on my hips. "It sounds crazy to me! Just crazy!"

"It *is*," she wept. "And I've been feeling so awful. I couldn't face you, April." She looked around for a place to put the presents while she felt for a handkerchief. I took them and she wiped her eyes and blew her nose.

"What does she mean, competition?" I asked.

"You're so pretty. *I* don't care, April, but *she* does. I guess it's because she's my mother," she said. She looked away. "And I'm not going back to Miss Parris next fall. Mom doesn't think I get enough training there. I have to take lessons in Bixby in some big school with a Russian name."

"I thought you were going to be a doctor."

"I am, I *am*," she cried. "If my mother will let me."

Suddenly I was so sorry for her that I wanted to cheer her up. "Come on and open the presents," I urged. We hoisted ourselves onto the stone wall. While she was tearing the paper off her presents I asked, "Was it a good party?"

"I guess." She stared down at the box on her knees. "But I felt so guilty."

"Well, don't be anymore," I said heartily. "My goodness, it didn't kill me to miss out on it. I mean, with the way Life *is*, not being invited to a birthday party is just about as unimportant as anything can be."

She said with admiration, "You think so old, April." She got down off the wall and so did I. I think we both knew it was a real parting.

"Look, April, I never let Phyllis talk about you. I don't even like her. She just hangs around to show off."

"Sure, I guessed that," I assured her. "What are you doing this summer?"

"I'm going to a camp where they talk French all the time, and ride horses."

"It sounds terrible," I said.

"It *is*. I hate it already." We both started laughing, and stopped as abruptly. "Well, so long," Sharon said.

"So long." We backed away, wanting to say something else but not knowing what, and then we each turned and went in different directions.

Five

After talking to Sharon I often thought about the strangeness of being disliked because I was pretty. Grown-ups were supposed to disapprove of you only when you were bad, but Mrs. Wilbur forbade Sharon to play with me because of my looks. Would more and more people turn against me for the same reason as I grew older?

I stopped worrying as we plunged into summer. After all, Phyllis wasn't bounding around town to annoy me. Wherever her camp was, she was probably organizing everything, including the counselors, and slept with a whistle strung round her neck.

This summer my mother began teaching me to sew. I had extra household chores and my dog-walking, my visits to my cousins, and the girls' return visits. (Brendan, going on fifteen now, had a job on a farm.)

One thing I hadn't expected was that I'd be having fun with Pam Hughes and Mary-Beth O'Brien. My looks didn't seem to bother their mothers or the girls themselves.

It all happened by accident. We knew each other at school but hadn't ever fooled around outside, until we sort of came together while we were watching the July Fourth parade. Then we made a date to take a bike ride the next day. After that, we called each other daily on the telephone, we giggled in hammocks, sunbathed in yards, were taken to the beach, to amusement parks, and special movies. I never talked about Sharon to them, though I often thought of her and was sorry for her in that far-off French-speaking camp.

Mary-Beth's ambition was to get married and have babies. I wanted babies too, but I was going to be a lawyer first.

Pam didn't want to marry — her parents fought a lot — and she was going to be an actress. She was skinny, all sharp knees and elbows, but she could imitate anybody you named around town, as well as television and movie actors. She could recite long poems from memory and enthrall us into silence. We used to think up suitable stage names for her. We also thought up husbands for Mary-Beth. The candidates changed from day to day, depending on what books we'd been reading or what we'd seen on television or in the movies.

My man would be a lawyer, which simplified the search, and he didn't have to be tall and handsome. One of my father's friends whom I liked very much was short and stocky. So somehow whenever I thought of that lawyer husband far off in the space-world of the future he always looked like Mr. Lindquist.

The last two weeks of August I went on a trip with my parents, and then there was the family picnic on Labor Day.

"It's been one of the best summers of my whole life," I told Brendan.

"See?" he said. And I did see. I'd survived the injury, I'd even managed to enjoy myself.

Sharon wasn't coming back to our school. Evidently her mother didn't want her to waste all the culture she'd gained in the summer. She'd be going to a private school in Bixby. Poor Sharon. Just the thought of such a life turned me sick and shivery in my stomach.

Mary-Beth, Pam, and I had firm plans for the sixth grade. My father called us the Three Musketeers, so we called ourselves the Tee Ems. The other kids named us the Three Morons, Three Messes, Three Mice, but nothing bothered me much on those September days.

Phyllis was back in the same room but even that couldn't upset me, now that I was one of the Tee Ems. She was tanned; she was very bossy, and wore around her neck a gold-colored whistle with her initials on it. A special award for something.

"Probably she was best at Kick the Can," said Pam.

"Or at blowing a whistle," Mary-Beth suggested. They'd been in Phyllis's gang when she'd first alighted in our midst from exotic Cleveland, but her charm hadn't lasted into the next grade for them.

At recess Phyllis kept blowing her whistle while her helpers ran around like sheep dogs trying to chivvy us into teams. Some really wanted to play, and a few were intimidated into it by the snapping at their heels.

Pam was athletic but didn't want to be bossed into it. Mary-Beth didn't care to have her shins kicked. I wouldn't be caught dead on one of Phyllis's teams. The three of us would rather watch the boys play soccer, especially Bobby Saxon.

Six

For the school concert this winter the two sixth grades were going to do an operetta written by Mr. Hanson, who taught the other sixth grade and was also band director. Everybody would have a chance to perform. If you didn't have a speaking part you could be one of the Merry Peasants dancing and singing in the street. And if you couldn't carry a tune, or had two left feet for dancing, you could be an old lady or gentleman doing your knitting or puffing on a clay pipe.

Naturally most of the boys wanted to be old gaffers with pipes instead of cavorting in circles with girls, but Mr. Hanson and Mrs. Davis were firm about assigning parts.

The entire sixth grade believed that Pam would be the heroine, because she was already known as a good actress. Pam believed it too, not in a conceited way but because she had faith in herself. There was really no choice, we thought. Besides, who else wanted to learn all those words and songs, and do some of them all alone up there, and others with a boy?

When I was picked, I nearly fainted. I sat there staring at Mrs. Davis, my face all cold

31

and my brain whirling like the windmill weathervane on our garage. She went on talking but I couldn't hear what she said, not even the boy lead's name.

Everyone was looking at me, but I could only feel Pam's eyes, even though I couldn't see her from where I sat. The bell rang, everybody rose, and I swung around to run to her, but she was hurrying out the door. Mary-Beth looked back at me with her round face all puckered up, and then she shook her head violently and ran after Pam.

Across the room Phyllis was grinning. She'd seen. Fury kept me from blubbering. I marched up to Mrs. Davis's desk. "What can I do for you, April?" she asked pleasantly.

"I don't want that part," I said, sounding blunt and brave. "Pam should have it."

"Why?" She didn't like this, and suddenly I didn't like her.

"Because Pam's an actress."

She laughed. "Oh, everybody goes through a stage of wanting to be a movie star. I did once, myself."

"But Pam really is an actress," I insisted. "You must know that! Look how she recites poems! She's got the talent, Mrs. Davis, and everybody knows it. This is *her* part."

"This is your part," she said. "Mr. Hanson and I agreed. You and Tim Wales will be splendid together. Pam can play your closest friend. If she's as good as you think, she'll act the part without complaining."

But she'll never be my friend again after

this, I thought. What could I say to convince this woman who had all at once become an enemy?

"No matter what Pam thinks she wants to be," she went on, "right now she's just a little girl like yourself, except that she's not — " She stopped short, and a giveaway flush came into her face.

"Pam can make anyone *think* she's beautiful," I said scornfully, "and that's what counts."

"I don't want to hear another word about this, April," she warned me. "Do you understand. Now run along."

I ran all the way to Pam's house but she wasn't home. Her mother was as nice as ever, so Pam couldn't have told her anything. "She's over at Mary-Beth's, dear," she told me. I wished I were brave enough to tell her then and there what had happened, but I wasn't.

It was deflating to find nobody home at Mary-Beth's. The car was gone, so Mary-Beth's mother had probably loaded everyone aboard and gone on an errand somewhere. Tired, tearful again, I went slowly home. I had this lonesome, shut-out feeling, and it was horridly familiar.

My mother was starting dinner and she asked me to scrub the potatoes for baking. While I scrubbed, I told her the story. I was a little more coherent than I'd have been earlier, but not much. When I finished I said, "So will you tell Mrs. Davis you don't want me to do the part? Then she'll give it to Pam."

"I understand how you feel," she said. "I used to run into those things too. But what reason would I give Mrs. Davis for not wanting you to play the part?"

"You have a reason!" I cried. "I've been telling you! If I do it Pam's never going to speak to me again, and Mary-Beth won't either!" I burst into tears. My mother let me go at it while she completed a few more preparations for dinner, then she told me to go wash my face and we'd talk. Which meant *she* was going to talk, or at least ask difficult questions. My father called it "reasoning." I didn't want to be reasoned with.

"Now, darling," said my mother. "Suppose I told Mrs. Davis I don't want you to do the part because *you* don't want to. What makes you so sure she'd then give the part to Pam?"

"She'd have to. Pam's the best one for it!"

"She didn't think so before. She could still give it to someone else. In fact, she probably would. Look, April, I know how you feel. I got picked for so many things that they began calling me Teacher's Pet, and I was fighting mad all the time." She started to laugh. She has a wonderful laugh and it's hard to resist, but I succeeded. "Once on a big day I came to school with every other front tooth blackened. I looked like a picket fence when I smiled, which was often. Then I had to go to the dentist to get the stuff off my teeth."

34

"I'm going to try that."

"No, you aren't. I used to fume and fuss about my looks, wishing for all kinds of things to happen to them, until a girl I knew was in a bad accident and her face was terribly scarred. After that I stopped fussing. And then the mean little things that others did and said didn't matter so much."

"Mother," I pleaded, "please get me out of this. They think I got it just because I'm — I'm — " I couldn't say the hated word. "Up till now they didn't care, they liked me because I was a good kid. But it's all changed now. Can't you *see*? I have to get out of it!" I howled, and stamped up to my room.

My father came home, and there was a hush downstairs which meant my mother was briefing him on the latest crisis. Sure enough, the tap came on my door, and I considered not answering, but didn't quite dare.

"Come in," I said with dignity, and composed my face for the cold war. He believed in the direct approach.

"It's time you stopped being temperamental. When you're a lawyer, are you going to throw a fit every time you win a case and say you don't deserve it? That the jury only went along with you because you're beautiful?"

He had a habit of coming up with unanswerable questions. While I was speechless, he said, "Now you are going to take that part, and you are going to do it so well that nobody can possibly say you got it only because you're prettier than Pam. It takes work, it takes thinking and imagination, it takes a brain, and you've got all the equipment. I'll expect you down in five minutes to set the table for dinner."

He left. And suddenly the part was possible for me. If I couldn't get out of it I might as well do the best job I could. I was warmed by a picture of Pam coming to me and saying, "You *were* best for it, and after all I've got plenty of chances ahead of me, so how about going to the movies with Mary-Beth and me?"

This got me through dinner with a good appetite. But I was glad it was a weekend, and I didn't have to get braced in the morning to be ignored by my ex-friends at school and laughed at by Phyllis.

It was all as I expected on Monday morning. I tried to make contact with Pam but she kept out of reach. I cornered Mary-Beth in the girls' room. "I had a real fight with old Davis," I told her. "And she won't let me out of it, and my parents won't, either. So it's not my fault."

"Yes, it is!" Her round face was pinched with distress. "When you're around, nobody else has a chance. You'll always get everything, because you're beautiful."

"But that's not my fault! Didn't you think I was a" — I could feel my voice thickening with tears — "a good kid all summer?"

"That's different," she said uncomfortably, and was rescued when someone came in and I had to move away from the door. I went out thoughtfully into the schoolyard, avoiding any would-be supporters. Phyllis and Pam were in a group of kids shooting baskets. I had stopped feeling like crying. What kind of friends were they, if they wouldn't forgive me for something I couldn't help, something I was born with? Something I'd give *them* if I could?

I was lucky to have my cousins, though probably if the girls and I went to the same school they wouldn't like me either, I thought sarcastically. It wouldn't make any difference to Brendan, though. He was a boy.

Seven

If I could only talk to Brendan, I kept thinking that afternoon. Why couldn't I go to see him? My mother wouldn't be home after school, she had a meeting. I knew how to get to St. Patrick's by bike, even if I'd never done it before. And Brendan should be having football practice there this afternoon.

Once home, I let Jones into the yard, had my snack while I changed into lined jeans and parka, and wrote my mother a breezy note. "Back soon. Love, A."

The afternoon was bright, calm, and cool. I had never taken such a long bike trip alone before, but I wasn't nervous until I was out on the highway. Whenever I heard a big truck coming, I went way over onto the shoulder and got off my bike and waited till the truck went by.

Once I was inside the gates of St. Patrick's, I knew where the athletic fields were and headed for them. But there was a lot of football practice going on, and I had to get up my courage to ask some older girls in track warm-up clothes if they knew where Brendan Snow was. I didn't have to explain further. They reacted the way most of us sixth-grade girls reacted to the name of Bobby Saxon.

They directed me to the field where the freshmen were. But then I couldn't pick him out of the helmeted figures shoving each other around. I was feeling very small and forlorn when a nice man said to me, "Looking for someone, Sis?"

"My cousin Brendan Snow, and it's urgent," I said in a trembly voice.

Brendan was given twenty minutes away from practice. He took off his helmet, and wrapped himself up in a huge blanket, and we sat in the empty bleachers. "Does your mother know you're here?" he asked sternly. "She doesn't, I can tell. Come on, I'm going to call her up."

"She's not home! And you have to hear something first!" I galloped through it so fast it's a wonder he made any sense of it. "Mrs. Davis says . . . Mother says . . . Daddy says . . . And Mary-Beth says . . . And Phyllis is *laughing*!"

I finished off by wailing, "And it's not my fault!"

I must have said it several times, because Brendan, leaning forward with his arms folded on his knees and watching me with blue eyes, said sharply, "Listen, you can't go through life saying 'It's not my fault' like a broken record. People get tired of it. I'm tired of it right now."

My eyes started to run over. "And don't start that either!" he ordered. "What good does it do? Maybe you enjoy it, but it would sure give those other guys a heck of a charge if they could see it. Your friend Phyllis would laugh herself sick."

"But — "

"But what? Listen, I know a little bit how you feel, I guess. But it happens to everybody, for one reason or another. You're not too young to get this through that thick little head of yours. Maybe it'll happen to you a lot because you're a beautiful kid. It makes you different, and the different ones stand out." He shrugged. "You might as well make up your mind you're not going to let it ruin your life."

"But I don't want people to hate me because of something that's — " I bit back *not my fault*. "I want them to like me because I'm a good kid."

"That's impossible. If everybody liked you you'd be some kind of — well, what kind of a lawyer will you be if you go around bleating, 'I want everybody to like me because I'm a good kid'?"

"You sound just like Daddy," I said icily.

"We're men. We think alike on important issues," he answered with a superior air.

"Don't be so pompous," I said. He laughed.

"But listen, Ape. The time'll come when there'll be plenty of people hanging around you, and you'll be beating your brains out then wondering if it's for the real you, or your looks. So you'd better toughen up and get on with your own life instead of wasting it worrying about what everybody else thinks of you, or you'll always be knocking your head against a stone wall."

I stood up. "Do you have friends, Brendan? Do you have a *best friend*?" I knew he did. He nodded at me, and I said, "Well, that's all I really want. I wouldn't care about everybody else."

"I'm your friend," he said, quite seriously.

"But you can't be my *best* friend. That has to be a girl. And every time I think I have one, or even two, like the way it was until this stupid operetta came up, it's ruined because of *the way I look*. And what I want to know is, will it always be like that? For the rest of my life?"

Brendan grinned. "Hey, maybe you'll grow out of your good looks. I've known some real pretty kids who turned into real messes. So cheer up. There's hope for you yet." He gave me a rough squeeze. "I don't mean to kid you. But you've just got to forget those jerks and have some fun."

They aren't jerks, and nothing's fun without them, I thought, but I didn't say it. "Well, I have to go home now," I said. "I'm sorry I interrupted your practice."

"Listen, I'm going to get one of the guys with a car to run you home."

"No, thank you," I said politely. "I like the ride."

"All right. I'll come a little way with you." We walked the bike. Boys and girls both called him by name and he was forever wav-

41

ing or throwing up his chin in answer. He was very popular, and I was proud to be seen with him, proud to have him for my cousin, wishing again he were my brother, even though he wouldn't say what I wanted him to say.

What *did* I want him to say? As if he could read my mind, he asked me that question at the gates.

"I don't know," I lied. "I guess you said what was right for somebody like you to say. You're almost grown up."

"Tell my dad that, will you?"

"And you've got loads of friends, and you're a boy, so you can't really know what it's like to be me."

"No," he agreed solemnly. "All I can tell you is that I'm on your side. Always have been, always will be. So hang in there; kid. And *be careful* on the way home. Stay way over."

"I will," I promised.

Eight

When I got home, both parents were very calm. I knew that kind of stillness. It meant they'd agreed beforehand not to lose their tempers with me. Fortunately Brendan had called my father as soon as I'd left for home, so they hadn't been calling all over town to locate me as dusk came on. But waiting for me to return to the house through home-going traffic hadn't been easy.

First I had to call the dog owners and apologize for being absent without notice this afternoon. Then I had to sit in a chair and *listen*.

When the lecture was over, I was told to wash up for dinner. With dignity I left the room, saying, "It'll probably make you very happy to know it didn't do me any good anyway. Brendan thinks just exactly like everybody else."

But he'd given me the hope of my becoming repulsive when I reached the pimply stage. I might get oily hair, and turn lumpy in the wrong places. I might even become permanently ordinary.

What a glorious dream!

While waiting for this, I might as well

buck up, so the part became precious to me. I had to have something to think about besides Pam and Mary-Beth when I woke up in the morning. (Pam had been given one of the "friend" parts. Mary-Beth was a Merry Peasant.) I worked hard, not to justify Mrs. Davis whom I blamed for my troubles, but so everybody would say I was good in spite of my looks.

The concert took place just before we broke for Christmas vacation, and the operetta was a great success. Everybody did well. I was so good, if I do say so myself, that the thought of a career on the stage gave the law a few hard nudges. In the shimmer and splendor of those two nights, as well as the matinees for the primary grades and the Nursing Home, almost everybody in the cast loved everybody else, and I became terribly popular. Even Mary-Beth gave me a quick "Hi!" and a grin when Pam wasn't there. But otherwise she was loyal to Pam and I admired her for that. I just wished someone was that loyal to me.

I made one last attempt when Pam and I came unexpectedly face to face one day after New Year's. I rushed into my speech. "I tried to make them give you the part, Pam, but nobody would let me out of it, so I had to do a good job, can't you see? For the school and everything."

She turned very white. "You didn't want it but you got it anyway. You get *everything* without even wanting it. You don't have to work for anything. It's not fair!"

She walked away. "*You're* not fair!" I shouted after her. I almost said, *It wasn't my fault!* But I remembered what Brendan said about the broken record. And I had discovered, all at once, that Pam couldn't forgive me for not making a mess of the part. I was cured of guilt. I was going to miss Pam and Mary-Beth like mad, but I was done with apologizing.

The rest of the school year was busy enough to keep me occupied. And I had a new client among my regulars — Rolfe, a Doberman. He was really a darling, but Jock and Jones were deeply suspicious of him, so I walked him alone, or with Gretchen, a big, happy, shaggy mongrel.

That summer Claire and Kathleen laughed a lot about Brendan and girls. He didn't have a girl, he fought shy of them, but they were giving him a hard time. I laughed about it too, feeling very safe as long as *he* was. But it bothered me sometimes. Suddenly the gap between us seemed so wide. Time was going too fast; it was rushing Brendan away from me.

Nine

A terrible thing happened that summer. Jones died.

I couldn't remember a time when Jones wasn't in my life. He was only two months younger than I, and we'd always celebrated his birthday. He had a hamburg cupcake all his own, and a small piece of the birthday cake the rest of us ate.

It wasn't fair that my fresh, frowsy Jones should suddenly have a heart attack. He had pills for a week but he grew rapidly worse, and they explained to me that he was suffering, he couldn't get better, and we must let him go. Dr. West would release him.

I fought. I howled, with my face in my pillow so Jones couldn't hear me. And then I had to give up because I couldn't stand seeing my Jones panting and trembling and not wanting to eat. My Jones who had always been so quick and so merry. My parents were going to let him go anyway, but they wanted me to understand and to say good-bye. They said I would be sorry afterwards if I didn't.

He was buried at the back of the yard near the weigelia bushes where he and I used to play house when we were little.

None of us wanted another dog, in spite of all the offers of free puppies. And I was ready to give up my clients, but after a few days I kept thinking that they missed *both* Jones and me. So I went, on my own; my parents didn't urge me. I cried a lot on some of those walks, out on the Cavendish road where I could keep to the edge of the fields and woods, and turn my wet face away from the road if a car came along.

One day I was out there with Rolfe when Matthew Page, the New Boy came along on his bike, and stopped. "Hi," he said without expression. "Hi, Rolfe." More enthusiasm for Rolfe, who returned it. Matt delivered the *Gazette* and had evidently got acquainted with Rolfe that way.

I was glad I'd already had my day's crying spell, but I was uncomfortable under those dark eyes that seemed to take in everything. "What are *you* doing out here?" I asked.

"Delivering a paper to the Simons." Those were the people who came to their lovely estate only in summer. "They pay extra for me to come way out here. Hey, I — " He stopped abruptly, twiddled with his handlebars, and then said in a rush, "I'm sorry about it."

He wouldn't say "your dog" and I appreciated that. "Thank you," I said, staring at the ground.

"I was thinking," he said. "When you go away with your folks for vacation, what about the dogs?"

"Well, I guess they get walks if anybody can take them, or they just stay in their yards. There aren't any other kids around who dog-walk."

"What about me?" He was very quiet about it. "I'm not trying to take your business, but I could replace you when you're gone two or three weeks, or if you're away other times. Then they wouldn't be cheated, and I could use the money."

"Well, gosh, Matt — I don't know." I was thinking, What if the dogs liked him better than they liked me? I couldn't stand that. Still, it would be good for them to have their walks when I was gone. I used to have guilty feelings about that.

"Well, if it's all right with the people, it's all right with me," I said finally. "You have to be patient, you know," I warned him. "Firm, but patient, and give them plenty of chances to smell."

"I will," he promised, stroking Rolfe's head.

"I'll write down something about each dog. You know, helpful hints."

"Thanks."

We smiled at each other, not very broadly, but it was an improvement on the impassive stares we usually exchanged. Then he went off on his bike, and Rolfe and I continued on our walk.

He worked out well as a replacement, and the dogs loved me as much as ever when I came back. Matt and I returned to mere nods in passing. I wondered if he talked to the dogs. Probably he did.

I was growing tall and my body was changing. And because of the experience with Pam, and losing Jones, my thinking was changing as well as my body. I now saw the old April as a tear-stained infant with a nose constantly stuffed up and eyes bleary from crying, or else fighting mad and yelling, "It's, not *fair*!" or "It's not *my* fault!"

Well, I wasn't a little kid any longer. I was starting junior high. I was on my way slowly (knowing my father's views on the subject) but inevitably to BOYS in my life.

Claire and Kathleen envied me. They were going away to the same convent boarding school their mother and her sisters had attended, and for the next six years — five in Kathleen's case, because she'd already done the seventh grade at St. Patrick's — they wouldn't go to school with BOYS.

I always thought of BOYS in capital letters, and collectively, because most of the individual boys I knew were an old story. I couldn't imagine getting excited over any of them, even the one to whom I'd sent an anonymous valentine in the fourth grade. And Bobby Saxon, and Tim Wales . . . I mean, what would we ever *talk* about?

But I was really happy about starting the seventh grade. This much bigger school would be a new adventure, far from the intimate world of the small neighborhood school and playground. For one thing Phyllis was going to be busy going out for everything (I hoped she'd get into cross-country running and get lost somewhere in the hinterlands), and I could stop suspecting that she was always watching and waiting for something bad to happen to me.

Ten

There were good programs in music, art, and drama, and that was what I was interested in. The drama side maybe meant Pam, but that last meeting with her had liberated me. She and Mary-Beth weren't in my home room. Phyllis was, but she was so excited about field hockey that I don't think she even saw me on those dazzling early days of the seventh grade.

The one thing I hated was gym, known as Fizz Ed. I wasn't lazy; I enjoyed all the stretching, limbering, and more strenuous exercises necessary in ballet, but even wearing a pale green leotard for Fizz Ed couldn't make me enjoy that. I walked miles with my dogs, biked more miles, and was a good swimmer, so why did I have to hurdle, vault, and balance?

I awoke deeply depressed on Fizz Ed day each week. The only consolation was that Phyllis wasn't in my gym class to watch me fail.

We were standing around one day watching a demonstration on the parallel bars and I was wondering how I could escape being called on, when I surprised an expression that must have been exactly like mine.

The girl stood across the circle from me, stocky and compact in a yellow leotard. She had short shiny black hair, thick and straight, worn in bangs. I knew her by name only; Lindy Warren. She was in my home room.

We were told to line up. Most of the others were eager, but I moved to the end of the line and there was Lindy trying to be the end too. "Maybe we'll get lucky and the bell will ring before it's our turn," I whispered.

Her sullen face shone in a sudden smile. "You hate it too?"

"I *despise* it!"

We didn't get lucky, but we got friendly. We ate lunch together that noon. Lindy had moved to town in the late summer, and her parents were both doctors. The town needed new doctors, and the Warrens were very warmly received, as the *Gazette* put it.

Lindy was so bashful that I was a lifesaver, and she was one for me too. She dogwalked and biked with me. We went to the library to work on projects together. We saw occasional Saturday afternoon movies, and started to learn tennis. We were excited to find out we shared favorite books. We were crazy about the same singers. She loved ballet but didn't think she'd be any good at it; I took her along to lessons, hoping she might change her mind. Her family was into cross-country skiing so I wanted cross-country skis for Christmas, and began dropping unsubtle hints in October. We planned on identical ice-skating outfits.

Sometimes Lindy came straight home from school with me, sometimes we went around to her house first. Her mother and father would be at their offices over in the Medical Arts Building, but her brother was usually at home. Ben was a tall thin senior, with long hair over his eyes, and occasional ugly outbreaks of acne. He was always eating when we came in, and he'd glare at us, and go upstairs with his hands full of food and drink.

"He's very unhappy," she told me matter-of-factly. "Brilliant, though. He's a terrific chess player. Pretty good tennis player too."

"What's he unhappy about?" I asked. "His pimples?"

She shrugged. "Oh — things. Maybe he'll get over it when he goes to college."

"Is he going to be a doctor?"

"No, it'll probably be something with computers. He likes machines better than people."

"If he doesn't like people, who does he play tennis with?"

"If you're a good player you can always get somebody to play with. They don't have to like *you*. It's the same with chess."

Lindy and I both made the high honor list for the first ranking period, and my father treated us to sundaes at Filippi's.

She came and spent a Friday night and

Saturday with me, and I made a return visit. The doctors were both there and they were very nice. There was lovely music on the stereo, and Ben and his father played chess. It impressed me, and I wondered if Brendan knew how to play chess. I'd seen him and Uncle Dan playing cribbage, and he was a fiendish wheeler-dealer at *Monopoly*, but chess was so *intellectual*.

Lindy stayed overnight with me again the Friday after Thanksgiving, and invited me to go to her house the next Friday night. After supper, while I was putting my pajamas and toothbrush into my canvas shoulder bag, my mother called the Warrens to be sure it was all right for me to go. She couldn't call Lindy's mother during the day because of her work.

Lindy answered. She said her mother was in the bathtub after a long hard day, and Lindy relayed my mother's inquiry and her mother's answer. Of course it was all right for me to come! They loved having me.

It was beginning to snow when my father drove me to the Warrens'. If the snow amounted to anything by morning, we were going coasting.

My mother had sent along a pan of mock cherry squares, with instructions to give half to the parents. The house was warm, bright, and welcoming, but no doctors were in sight.

"Where are your father and mother?" I asked, carefully unpacking the squares.

"Oh, I guess maybe you didn't hear," said

Lindy. "A bus skidded off the Cavendish road, and they brought so many people into Emergency most of the doctors in town are at the hospital. They'll be back later. Hey, these are neat."

"What's neat?" said Ben, appearing in the doorway. He scowled at us, took a couple of squares, and disappeared upstairs.

"He's studying. Cramming for his college boards," said Lindy. "Boy, is he ever mean these days! . . . What'll we do? Want to watch the Friday night movie? Play cards? Play records?"

We chose the movie, loading up with squares and milk, and settling down to enjoy ourselves. The movie was horribly, deliciously creepy. "They don't let me watch these," Lindy said happily, "because I dream. But I won't tonight, because you'll be there."

"Besides, we'll be talking half the night," I said.

Later we made salami and pickle sandwiches. When the movie was over at half-past ten the doctors hadn't yet come home, and it was snowing hard. Yawning and bleary-eyed, stuffed with food, we watched the last half of a police show we didn't really care about.

I said, "Let's listen to the eleven o'clock news, maybe they'll tell about the accident." But just then Ben came running down the stairs and Lindy quickly turned off the television.

Ben looked in at us, his hair standing out

in all directions. "Did you watch that movie?" he asked Lindy.

"What movie?" she asked.

"Well, if you wake April up with some of your screeches that'll be the end of a beautiful friendship. You two had better get to bed." He went to the kitchen. I was ready to go to bed, if not to sleep. I'd eaten so much I thought I'd feel better lying flat.

We brushed our teeth and settled down in Lindy's twin beds. We kept the light on for a while, lying there dreamily talking — at least I dreamily talked. Lindy seemed edgy, fidgety. I didn't know if it was from the movie or all the food or both.

Eleven

Perhaps she was nervous about her parents driving home in the storm. There were a couple of tricky hills between the hospital and here. I asked her.

"Well, kind of," she admitted.

"Why don't you call up and see if they've left yet?"

"Maybe I will," she said. "I was just thinking I ought to get a Tum or something. I'm about to have the burps." She put on her robe and slippers. "I'll be right back."

"Okay." She left the door open, and I could hear faintly the FM music Ben liked while he was studying. I tried to hear Lindy telephoning the hospital from her parents' room across the hall, but I couldn't. Maybe she was getting her anti-burp medicine first. In your own house you know every creak, but this house seemed to have no creaks. Except for Ben's far-off music, there was no sound of humanity, and they had no pets.

It was so weird and creepy I was about ready to get up and look for her, except that I had myself half-scared to step over the threshold.

My scalp began to tighten. Lying flat

wasn't doing anything for my stomach. I lay rigid, staring at the slot of dark hall beyond the open door.

The music had stopped. There was a lull in the storm, and even a gust of wind would have seemed friendly. When something tall suddenly appeared in the doorway I yelped with shock, and bounced up, then recognized Ben and sagged with relief. "Oh boy," I breathed. "Wow . . . where's Lindy?"

"She'll be back." He shut the door behind him and came to the foot of the bed. "Everything all right?"

"Yes, if Lindy is. She felt sick, and I guess she's worried about your folks."

"They're all right, I checked. She's getting Alka Seltzer." He spoke in a fast toneless voice, without taking his eyes off me. He must be awfully tired, I thought.

"Did you get a lot of studying done?" I asked chattily. "I'm glad I don't have to think about college boards for a good long time yet."

He sat down on the side of the bed, staring hard at me.

I saw for the first time that his eyes were light brown with a dark edge around the iris. There was a new rash of angry red pimples on his chin. I moved a few inches toward the other side of the bed. My throat felt very strange. I tried to speak but had to swallow first.

"I'd better go see if Lindy's all right."

"She's all right." Suddenly he leaned across

me and planted his hand on the other side of my legs, pinning the bedclothes down hard, and bringing his face very close to mine. I leaned back as far as I could and his face followed mine. I could smell his oily hair and his clothes and the salami he'd been eating.

"All I want is a little kiss," he said thickly.

I exploded in panic and rage. I delivered a punch to that arm stretched across me, and the imprisoning hand flew up as he grunted with pain and surprise. Then I threatened him with both fists, at the same time kicking violently at him through the bedclothes.

He swore and grabbed at my flailing fists, but I seized the bedside lamp. "You get out of here!" I yelled. "If you touch me, I'll brain you!"

He ran, slamming the door behind him. I jumped up to lock it. I was shaking, I felt sick to my stomach, I wanted to go home at once. But it would mean waking my parents and bringing my father out into this slippery storm.

Then I heard them in the hall. Ben's voice was jumpy and arrogant. "You don't think you'll get paid for this, do you?"

"I got her here." Lindy's voice trembled. "That's all I promised. You'd better give me my five dollars or I'll tell them about it."

"Yeah? And how will that make *you* look?"

"If she tells her father and mother, ours will know anyway." She sounded miserable. But I wasn't a bit sorry for her. "You traitor," I whispered. "You liar and sneak."

I went back to bed wishing I could call Brendan. Once I heard his voice I would feel like *me* again, not someone cut off forever from all dear, safe, daylight things. I huddled in a little ball under the bedclothes trying to get warm.

The doorknob rattled, and Lindy said, "Let me in."

"NO."

"He's not here."

"I don't believe you."

"Please, April," she choked. "I swear he's not here!"

I got up and unlocked the door, but I picked up the doorstop just in case. She came in sidewise through the narrow gap I allowed her and I locked the door again. I went back to bed and turned to face the wall.

She put out the light, and the sound of the storm filled the dark room. I flopped over on my back and said, "Why, Lindy?"

"I wanted the money." She was weepy. "And I didn't think it would do any harm."

"What if your father and mother came in while he was bothering me?"

"They won't be home. They're gone for the weekend."

"Then it was all a lie about the bus accident, and about your mother taking a bath and everything?"

"Yes, they'd already gone," she said drearily.

The enormity of it left me speechless for a moment. Then I said, "You must have wanted money awful bad to pull such a dirty trick." She didn't say anything. "What did you want it for?"

"I just *wanted* it. For myself. In case I saw something I wanted to buy."

"You get a bigger allowance than I do!"

"I didn't think it would hurt you. If you were a good kid you'd let him kiss you." She was working herself up. "I suppose you think you're so beautiful you're sacred, like some goddess. Nobody should even *breathe* on you."

"Oh yeah? Anybody doesn't have to feel *sacred* to be choosy about some things. And what's he want to fool around with a young kid for, anyway? Is he *crazy*?"

"He can't make it with girls his own age. All he wanted was a *kiss*! What's a kiss, for heaven's sake?"

"Hey, I'm not stupid. I didn't just come into town on a load of parsnips." Brendan used that phrase and I always thought it was pretty snappy.

"I suppose you'll run to your Mummy and Dada about this," Lindy said sarcastically.

"Wouldn't you, if somebody you thought was your friend did something like this?"

She started to cry, and I went on. "Did you ever really like me or was it all for Ben? I mean, to get money?"

She cried harder. I guess she saw then where it was all leading. Where it had already led.

Twelve

I fell asleep after a while and woke up to sunny silence. Lindy was still asleep, or pretending to be. I dressed fast, frantic to get out before she could speak to me. Picking up the heavy doorstop, I let myself out and darted across the hall to the bathroom and locked myself in. The house had the strange bleak stillness of other people's houses in the morning when you're homesick.

Still carrying the doorstop, I sneaked past Ben's door. I had to put my weapon down while I got into my boots and jacket, and I left it on the stairs where, if I was lucky, Ben would trip over it when he came down. He might fall against something and get a black eye, which would be from me even though he'd dodged too fast last night.

And then I was out in the bright glittering morning, running down the middle of the newly plowed street under the great arches of the bare elms and the deep intense blue of the sky. Hardly anyone was stirring except some early shovelers, and a few dogs, who barked at me. I barked back, joyous, laughing, *free*. The nightmare was over.

My parents were having breakfast. Never had I beheld them with such rapture. How handsome *he* was in his old slacks and faded plaid shirt, with his dark red hair trying to be wavy if he'd let it, and the cleft in his chin and the dimple in one lean cheek, and his aristocratic (*I* thought) profile. And my mother — *she* was the beauty I'd never be, with the high fair head, and the golden-brown eyes almond-shaped under the delicate slim feathers of eyebrows that arched now with astonishment at the sight of me.

"Hi, I'm starved!" I announced over the poetry charging around in my soul. "Are you having *pancakes*?"

"Didn't you have breakfast over there?" my father asked. "I thought you were going coasting this morning."

"All the stuff we ate last night didn't agree with Lindy's stomach," I said glibly. "So she was still asleep this morning. Everybody was. So I just came home."

I began cooking my pancakes. "What I would really like," I said to the griddle, "is to go out to the farm to coast. . . . I could take the bus, and use one of their sleds —"

"The girls won't be home now until Christmas," my mother reminded me.

"I wouldn't care." Brendan would probably come home at noon to eat, and I could tell him about last night. I had to tell somebody. I wasn't going to tell my father and mother.

"What about the big research job you've been talking about for two weeks?" asked my father. "This would be a good weekend for that."

I held up both hands. "Daddy, I will start my research this weekend, okay? After I shovel the front steps and walk, and take care of the dogs. I will spend the whole afternoon in the library, returning my books and taking notes."

I spent almost two hours in the library, and when I came out the street lights were on, shop windows bright, the Christmas decorations all aglow. I saw Ben standing on the corner across from me. I froze. I could remember how it was last night, my uneasiness turning into fear, and then panic when he pinned me down.

But he was looking the other way and hadn't seen me yet, and then he walked off around a corner.

I got Brendan at supper time, using the upstairs extension, but he was in a hurry. He was going skiing with some friends by moonlight. What a glamorous, carefree life some people led! "I want to tell you something," I said. "It's important."

"Okay, Ape, I'll try to fix it up soon. Are you all right?"

I was, the instant he asked me. "Sure. But it's something I have to tell somebody. Urgently," I added, to sound impressive.

"Sometime this week then. Keep your cool."

Monday Lindy didn't come to school, which was good. Also, the junior high wasn't near the senior high; I didn't want to see Ben even at a distance. That day I didn't even mind Phyllis. At noon I ate lunch with a bunch from our old school. When we were at our lockers in the afternoon, one of them said to me, "Hey, April, come on downtown with us to look in the stores!"

"Sure!" I said eagerly. I wanted to go more than anything else I could think of, to be just one of a gang laughing and window-shopping on Main Street.

But when we came out, there on the sidewalk was Brendan. "Oh, there's my cousin!" I exclaimed in happy surprise.

They looked admiringly at him. He was so big and handsome with his bare black head and blue eyes; he wore one of those Irish-fisherman sweaters under his blue jacket. Proudly I invited the others to come and meet him.

He called each girl by her name as I said it, smiled at her as she were the only one there, and they could hardly tear themselves away.

"So long, April! So long, Brendan!" they chorused. The most daring one called back, "Come again, Brendan!"

"Gosh, if you were around all the time I'd never have any trouble finding a friend," I told him. "The trouble is, I'd know it was because of you."

"And my fatal charm's no more my fault

than you're to blame for yours. Ain't life awful for us Beautiful People!"

"Yes!" I said ferociously. We sat in his fourth-hand VW and I told him what had happened. He flushed angrily.

"I guess I'll have to talk to this guy," he said. "Lean on him a little."

"I don't want you to hit him!" I exclaimed. "I just wanted to tell you because I have to tell *somebody* and you're the best."

"Why don't you want me to belt the creep?"

"Because it would make an awful mess! His father and mother are really nice."

"If they're that nice, how come they have a pair of kids like those two?"

"I dunno," I said. "And I didn't know she felt that way about money. I'd have given her five dollars out of my bank, if she'd asked me."

"For Pete's sake, don't ever start *that*. A nut like her could drain you dry. There's something really kooky about anybody so crazy about money she'll do anything to get it. Listen," he said grimly. "Promise me one thing, or I'll twist your head right around so you'll have to walk backwards the rest of your life. If he ever bothers you in *any* way again, you let me know."

"I promise," I said solemnly.

He looked long and silently at me and I stared back, wondering what he was thinking, if it was still rage with Ben that turned him so somber. Then he shook his head, and

66

turned the ignition key. "I'll take you home, or do you want me to drop you downtown where the other kids are?"

"No, I'd better go home and take the dogs out before it gets dark."

Thirteen

On the way he said, "I still think you ought to tell Uncle Tom and Aunt Karen."

"No! I told you why I don't want them to know. Besides, the way Daddy feels about boys, if he ever heard about this I'd be locked up till I'm thirty. I'll be having my first date when I'm a middle-aged woman, for heaven's sake!"

Brendan guffawed, and I was indignant, but I knew he'd keep my secret.

While I was out with the dogs, I felt so much better that I could even think of Lindy without this nasty feeling in my stomach. Suddenly I realized that she must have been waiting since Saturday morning for the axe to fall, and she could be physically sick about it.

When I came home, my mother had gone next door for a few minutes, so it seemed meant that I should call Lindy. Not that she deserved it. She sounded scared, and I was glad. "Don't worry," I said curtly. "I'm not telling. I don't want to make a mess for our parents. I just want to forget it." I hung up.

Lindy came back to school the next day. We spoke if we had to, but stayed well apart.

There was so much going on these weeks before Christmas that if our separation was noticed it didn't take up much attention.

After three days my mother asked me where Lindy was, and I told her we'd had a fight. Tactfully she didn't ask the cause. All she said was, "I was afraid that would happen, you were together so much. Everyone needs more than one friend, April. Spread yourself around a little more."

I was glad to have Christmas to think about with all its sweet excitements and surprises. But it was also my first Christmas without Jones. He'd always had a fresh bone, gift-wrapped and placed under the tree early Christmas morning. Jones's passionate plunge among the packages in search of his own was one of the traditions of our holiday, like the lumpy stockings hung from the mantel. I think we three all missed Jones like mad that morning.

My main New Year's resolution was that I'd have no bad feelings toward anyone, including Lindy and Ben. On the first day back at school my resolution got a good workout, because Phyllis and Lindy were very chummy. The black head and the yellow one were close before school, between classes, and at lunch. It looked as if Phyllis moved in whenever I separated from someone. But it didn't bother me this time. In fact I was amused to remember how I'd once thought Phyllis so sophisticated because she came from Cleveland, Ohio.

Then one rainy morning before classes Phyllis stopped by my desk. I looked up. Sweetly, I hoped. "Hi," I said, which was probably the first time I'd spoken directly to her since the meeting outside the Elm Street gate.

She smiled. "What about you and Ben Warren when his parents were away?"

If I'd been less shocked I'd have laughed and said, "What are you talking about? Are you *crazy*?"

But this dagger-plunge out of nowhere brought it all back, the terror and betrayal of that night. I went sick to my stomach and trembly all over. I could only stare back at Phyllis, hoping I wouldn't throw up right there on my desk.

She laughed and went on. I was burning and freezing at the same time. The girl across the aisle said, "What was *that* about?"

"I don't know," I mumbled.

"You look kind of sick." She whispered to the boy ahead of her, who looked around at me, and then quickly away.

It was only the beginning of a hideous week. There were whispers in corners, broken off when I walked by. Snickers followed me in the schoolyard, from boys and girls both. I began to believe I was being talked about every time I saw two people together.

That wasn't so, of course. There were plenty of kids who were too busy to give the gossip any attention. But as it blossomed I didn't know whom to trust.

Phyllis jeered triumphantly at me in my dreams. Because I looked strained and tired each morning, I told my parents I was worrying about my part in the new play the Drama Club was giving, and they said I'd better stop being that anxious or I'd have to leave the club.

When I was supposedly doing homework in my room, I'd be staring into my mirror, saying to the girl framed there, "I hate you. You're to blame for everything."

And with her mouth firm, her chin up, and her thin nose arrogant, the one dimple in hiding, she'd gaze back at me from the long sea-green eyes as if I'd never in a million years guess what she was thinking.

Was that how I appeared to others? I wondered. So that I puzzled or even infuriated them?

"Green eyes, greedy gut! Eat all the world up!" Phyllis used to chant at me in the old days. No wonder she'd do anything to strike away that expression. Feeling like a lifeprisoner, I would finish off my revery by making one of my most horrible grimaces — an art form brought to perfection in competition with Kathleen and Claire years ago.

There were three mysterious phone calls. My parents each answered one, and were hung up on. I answered one, and got the dirty language. I was alone in the house, and the caller must have known it. I threw up my afternoon snack, locked all the doors, and struggled against a powerful desire to throw myself into parental arms, or call Brendan.

What could Brendan do besides listen to me? As for my parents —

"Ignore these people," my father always advised loftily whenever I complained that someone was mean to me. He'd feel different about obscene phone calls, but what could he do, any more than Brendan? And I didn't want to hit my mother with it.

All that nightmare week, I hung around the school library after classes, pretending to look up material so almost everybody would be gone by the time I left. On Friday I was there, hunched over my book without reading a word of it, when someone spoke softly behind me.

"April."

I jumped. It was Pam. She pulled out a chair and sat down. She was pale under her freckles, and obviously braced to get something over with. "I don't believe it," she said. "Mary-Beth doesn't. A lot of kids don't."

"Thanks, Pam," I said. My nose stuffed up.

She said in an embarrassed rush, "Lindy started it, but Phyllis is right in there pitching."

"Started *what*?" I whispered. "I just get these wise-cracks and these stupid snickers. I don't even know what they're talkig about!"

"Lindy says the reason she's not your

friend anymore is because when you came to stay overnight at her house, she went to brush her teeth and Ben went into the room with you and you locked her out of her own room and he didn't come out for a long time. . . . Are you going to *faint*?" She was frightened.

"No. I'm pale with rage. What more?"

"She says you only made believe you're her friend to get next to Ben, and she never knew you were that kind of girl, and her parents don't want her to associate with you."

"Anything more?" I asked grimly.

"She says all you think about is your looks and getting men with them. . . . Maybe if you were just ordinary, people wouldn't pay any attention to her at all. But they're — well, you're different, April. You stand out. They're jealous, some of them." She was blushing. "The way I was. But not now."

"I'll tell you what really happened."

She didn't take her eyes off my face as I talked. When I finished she said solemnly, "I believe you. And I'll tell your side of it. But who's going to tell it at the high school? That rotten Ben's telling even more lies."

"Maybe I'll just kill him myself," I whispered.

Fourteen

It was more than a month since that awful night. Why had Lindy waited to start the New Year off like this? And I wasn't so naïve that I couldn't imagine what Ben was saying.

I sat for a long time at the library table, my head in my hands, trying to get over the shaking inside me. I was still the same ordinary kid who liked dogs and was crazy about cross-country skiing. But somebody was trying to turn me into something cheap and soiled.

I slammed the book shut and returned it to its right place on the shelf. By now there were only two or three people left in the library. As I walked out, a boy looked up past a stack of reference books and gave me a thoughtful nod.

Matthew Page. Matt. New Boy. I jerked my chin up in response and hurried out. "And what are you thinking about?" I asked him silently. "Nothing but your books, I guess. Well, that's a nice change from the usual around here."

I went home and collected the dogs. Jock was out of town at a dog show, but I had Lissa the Aussie, Sancho the cockapoo, and a pair of tireless pugs named Edward and Lola. I'd take Rolfe and Gretchen later that day.

I headed for the Cavendish road. We were having the January thaw and there was no wind, the sky was soft, the sun gentle. It felt like early April, as if the traces of snow in the fields were the last signs of winter. I could *think* out here, meandering along with the dogs. I felt safe and clean in their company.

I decided the one thing I would do was to tell Lindy what I thought of her. At least I'd have that satisfaction. The minute I got home I'd call her up and burn her ears off. As for Ben, the most personal satisfaction I could get would be to kick his teeth in, and that didn't look possible.

I was almost out to the Simon estate by now. I crossed the road to go back on the other side, and a car shot past me from the direction of town, blasting the horn. It made me jump, and rush the dogs toward the ditch and almost fall into it myself. The car braked with screaming tires, made a U-turn, and came back on the wrong side of the road, moving slowly toward me.

The Aussie braced her legs and barked furiously at it. The pugs joined in. Sancho pranced happily, not suspicious. I pulled the dogs along, difficult because Lissa wasn't going to turn her back on the enemy and the pugs knew by her bark that something was wrong. There were hoots of laughter from the three high school boys inside the car.

"Sorry, Sweet Stuff! Hey, watch it there! Don't bump the little nose! Hey, what's old Ben got that we haven't?"

And so forth and so on as the car crawled beside me. I won't cry, I won't cry, I kept saying to myself. For the first time I longed for lots of traffic on this road. Deserted, it lay before me as if it would never reach town again. I tried not to hear the things they said, but they whistled to the dogs who pulled around to see and to bark, and almost tripped me up. The boys said worse and worse things. I was sick, terrified, and *murderous*.

What if they stopped and got out? Oh, why hadn't I taken Rolfe and Gretchen first instead of the little dogs? The mere sight of the Doberman would have kept them in the car.

A truck went by on the other side. The driver must have thought I was enjoying the attention, and with my hands full of leashes I couldn't signal for help.

Then a car came barreling around the curve ahead and straight at us. The boys shouted and swore as it bore down on them. They were creeping, but this one was coming fast, and they were on the wrong side of the road. Their driver stepped on the gas and tried to swing across the road as the stranger came to a shrieking stop, barring their way.

I didn't recognize the shabby Chevy, but I was going to shout at the driver and beg him to take me home. I didn't care if he *was* a stranger. I was already too frightened by people whose faces I knew. Besides, Lissa could deliver a good hard bite even if she didn't look it.

The driver got out. It was Brendan, with a note pad in his hand. He looked awfully big.

I stood there shaking, my mouth open, while he wrote down their registration number. They acted stunned, not moving or speaking in their car. Then he waved his arm at them and said, "Get out of here. *Move it!*"

They moved. Rapidly. He drove to my side of the road and parked on the shoulder. When he got out and came toward me I was immediately defended by three dogs, but not Sancho, who loved everybody without discrimination and would have shown a burglar where all the silver was kept.

"Stop it, it's Brendan," I told Lissa, and burst into tears. Tactfully Brendan fooled with the dogs until I could mop myself up. Then he loaded us aboard, all the dogs tremendously excited in the back seat. We drove as far as the Simon estate and turned into the driveway and parked.

I told him what had been going on, and he understood why I didn't want to get the parents mixed up in it. But he gave me a good bawling out for not letting him know the minute the smears started.

"I guess I didn't lean on old Ben hard enough," he said. "This time I'll crunch a little."

"Break all his fingers, I don't care," I said

bitterly. "What are you doing here, anyway? Whose car is that?"

"Mine. I traded the VW and I haven't had a chance to fix her up yet." Fondly he patted the wheel. "What I'm doing here is, I had funny feelings all day. I didn't know whether it was the flu coming on or if I've got psychic powers from my Irish great-granny who could read tea leaves."

I giggled.

"Anyway, I drove over from school, nobody was home, so I spoke to Mrs. Comstock and she said you'd gone out with the dogs, so I chased you. And a good thing. I'll take care of these clowns."

"How?" I demanded.

"Find out which one owns the car, first. I could report the driver to the police, but I guess I'll go see him myself and threaten a little. Same with Ben. Where'd he be this time of day?"

"At school, maybe working in the lab or playing chess. Or at home. Or," I added, "he *might* be playing tennis at the Y."

"I'll track him down. Never fear, Brendan Bloodhound's here." I laughed so hard the dogs got carried away too, and Brendan said, "Hey, it wasn't *that* funny. You aren't going to freak out on me, are you?"

"I'm just foolish with relief, I guess. But what can you threaten *with*? They could gang up on you sometime."

"I can threaten with the entire football

squad of St. Pat's," he said blandly. "The perfect deterrent, you might say."

"Fabulous!" I breathed. "And I can take care of Lindy and Phyllis."

"Want me to give you a crash course in karate?"

"Nope. Phyllis probably knows it already."

"Well, listen, don't let 'em corner you. Want me to drive you around to Lindy's and wait outside?"

"No, you go tend to the others." I was full of fight and confidence now. Where the Cavendish road joined the foot of our street I asked him to let me off so the dogs could walk the rest of the way. "Nobody'll dare bother me now."

"All right. Look, I'll call tonight. I'll think of some legal question to ask Uncle Tom, for a paper I'm doing, and then I'll get a chance to tell you what happened. Okay?"

"Okay!" I felt I could follow him through life saying "Okay!" to anything he suggested.

The dogs and I jogged all the way to Lindy's. I tied them outside and walked in at the back door. I was lucky. Phyllis was there too, just through with basketball practice. They were stuffing themselves in the kitchen.

Phyllis laughed out loud when she saw me. She was wearing her gold whistle around her neck. Lindy's face was pinched, her eyes had a funny stare. "What do you want?" she asked faintly.

"To shut you up," I said. "Both of you. I

guess you never heard of the laws about libel and slander. Defamation of character. Harassment. You never heard of writs of mandamus. Amicus curiae. Nolo contendere." I leaned forward, pointing a finger, and hissed, "*Habeas corpus!*"

Lindy's eyes were like black glass marbles. Phyllis's tongue touched her dry lips. "They're all waiting for you," I whispered. "All I have to do is tell the right people."

I turned around and walked out before Phyllis could speak. Lindy didn't look as if *she* ever would. I went quickly away. The Latin legal phrases were pure nonsense in this case, but they didn't know it.

I got home in a very happy condition, and took a good walk with Rolfe and Gretchen around local streets. Dinner that night tasted better than anything had tasted for a long time.

Fifteen

The boy who was driving the car that day was so afraid of Brendan's going either to the police or his parents, or both, that he promised he'd never bother me again or even mention my name.

As for Ben, Brendan didn't hit him, and wouldn't have; Ben was so scared. "He's a little sick in the head, Ape, if you can see it that way. He has to brag about something to make himself important to the other guys."

"And Lindy made up stories to make herself important?"

"Sure. And she got plenty of attention, didn't she? She was important enough when she was buddying with the prettiest girl in school, but when that girl dropped her she had to make herself important in another way."

"Now you put me in the wrong." I was uncomfortable.

"No! What else could you do when those two ganged up on you? She had your friendship but she abused it. And if Ben had all his marbles he wouldn't be chasing little girls, if you'll pardon the expression."

"I do," I said humbly. "What I can't figure

out is how they can be so — so the way they are, when the doctors are so nice."

"It happens, Ape."

Then I said, "I wonder if the doctors ever wonder where I am."

There were a couple more phone calls, but I hung up on them at once. Nobody else bothered me on the road. As for the kids who'd joined in the talk at school, they were soon thinking about something else.

Phyllis had dropped Lindy fast. I didn't know if it was because of my visit or if she'd have done it anyway — Lindy wasn't into any kind of athletics — but now Lindy was alone. I hated to see her hurrying along with her head down as if she didn't want her thinking to be interrupted. I'd been through it myself.

But I could never make up.

Mandy Mackay was one of the girls who hadn't seemed to pay any attention to the gossip. She and her chums were the ones I'd been going with that day when Brendan met me outside, and now they asked me again. Mandy's father was the mayor, the kind of man they call a live wire, and Mandy was the same way, so busy you wondered how she ever got any schoolwork done. She had run for class president but lost out to Tim Wales.

She shrugged. "Of course, it *had* to be a boy. Sex discrimination. Well, that's on its way out. . . . What's junior high anyway? I'm on my way to being president of the senior class and I've got four years to campaign in."

"Then she'll start campaigning to be our first woman mayor by the time she's twenty-one," Kim Pierce kidded her.

She bristled. "Don't you think it's time we had a woman mayor?"

We'd have cheered except that we were having hot chocolate in Filippi's. Teresa's treat; she was the Filippis' granddaughter. There was something about the place that made it easy to be ladylike.

This was when I was invited to a Valentine party, an all-girl affair because Mandy's father was like mine about BOYS.

Ten of us were taken out to the Snow Bowl in Mandy's brother's van for moonlight skating, and then back to her house for a feast. Afterwards we played records and practiced disco dancing.

You couldn't say I now had a gang, because we had different activities both in school and outside. But we ate together and sometimes I went to basketball games with Teresa because Mandy and Kim were cheerleaders. They really seemed to like me for myself.

When school was out, our room had a picnic to celebrate at Mandy's family's summer house on Silver Lake. I wore my oldest Levis and the Mickey Mouse T shirt somebody'd brought me from Disneyland.

The mayor didn't come, having the town to run, but his wife was there, of course, and a couple visiting from New York. The man from New York was fat and bearded, and wandered around draped with cameras and light meters. Occasionally he took a picture. He had no expression that I could see except utter boredom.

The Mackays had brought their dog out too, a young golden retriever named Kate. Kate and I wrestled a bit, till she rolled over on her back and waved her feet in the air while I scratched her belly.

"Hello!" It was the man from the house. He looked less bored. "You two are having so much fun, can I snap you?"

"Sure," I said, dodging Kate's tongue again, and paid no more attention to him. Kate saw to that. I did know that he went on snapping away at us from various angles. Sometimes he said quietly, "Look this way, will you?"

Once he got down on one knee, just out of Kate's reach, and whistled to keep her attention. "Rest your chin on her head and look thoughtful," he said. "Dreamy. You know that Longfellow saying, 'The thoughts of youth are long long thoughts.' So show me."

It was like Drama Club. I showed him, and he said softly, "Perfect." He took several shots.

His wife and Mrs. Mackay came around the corner.

"What are you up to, Philip?" His wife sounded amused.

"He's got some smashing pictures of Kate," I told them.

"What are you going to be when you grow up?" Philip asked me.

"A lawyer," I said promptly.

"Good grief." Philip shut his eyes and slapped his forehead. I think he'd have said something stronger except for my tender years. Then he looked at me and said, " 'If eyes were made for seeing, then Beauty is its own excuse for being.' "

"Emerson," I said. "Well, I guess I'll go find the kids."

"What's your name, dear?" Philip asked me. "I'll send you some prints. Your parents might like them."

"Oh, thank you!" I said happily. "My name's April —"

"April," he said. "It's perfect. Just 'April.' Can't you see it?" he asked the women. "She has exquisite bones. Skeleton by Cartier."

"Go along if you want to, April," Mrs. Mackay said. "I'll give him your address."

Sixteen

At dinner that night I told my parents about the man taking pictures, and laughed again about my "exquisite bones." A few nights later the Mackays and my parents were at the same affair, and Mandy's mother told them this man was her cousin, and a respected photographer. He'd taken many pictures of Mandy and her brothers, and he'd enjoyed photographing me with the dog. That was all there was to it.

It was a super summer, never dull for a moment. I made some new clothes. For work, I had my dogs, and the extras like giving baths, combing burrs out of ears, trips to the vet, and helping to give medicine. I had to do extra chores at home. (Not for pay, unless you called my modest allowance pay.) Then I grandmother-sat one afternoon a week while Mrs. Andrews played tennis. The old lady was quite lame and I was supposed to get things for her or, if she wanted to move around, be right there so I could call for help in case she fell. Her eyes weren't good for fine print so I used to read to her. Sometimes we sorted her old photographs, and she told me stories about the people in them.

The Andrews house was one of the places where New Boy mowed the lawn and clipped the hedge, and he always seemed to be there when I was.

"Odd, isn't it?" old Mrs. Chisholm said mischievously.

"Kind of," I said in all innocence. "The way he moseys around you'd think he'd never get anything done, but he always does. He must be like the tortoise. Slow but steady."

"He's not so slow," she said. "He always gets done in time to sit a while with us."

Which was true. He'd come up on the shady porch and have lemonade and cookies. Mrs. Chisholm taught us old-fashioned card games like euchre and bezique. Matt had a real poker face until he won, and then this sudden merry grin transformed him completely. But it didn't happen too often; Mrs. Chisholm and I were pretty sharp card players too.

The rest of the time I was one of a gang with Mandy, Kim, Teresa, and Sheila. The Frightful Five, my father called us, and we were proud of it. We were always laughing, talking, singing. We were all over town on our bikes, and we had long days on the beach below the Mackay house at Silver Lake. If boys collected around us, that made a special kind of fun. None of us at that point wanted to be alone with a boy. So we were safe in a crowd, and *so* original and witty.

When the photographs finally came, it was quite exciting. Kate looked beautiful. And there I was wearing my old Levis and my Mickey Mouse T shirt, my hair blowing every which way. But my face — I looked like some tall slender stranger whose thoughts were absolutely unknown. It was as if the photographs disguised me, or showed me playing a part.

Mr. Latimer also wrote to my parents and they let me read the letter. "Just don't get above yourself," my father warned me. "No delusions of grandeur."

"Yep, I know. Handsome is as Handsome does," I chanted.

Mr. Latimer wanted to make a model out of me. They must, he wrote, realize that I had a distinctive beauty and an instinctive poise, and already possessed the indefinable qualities that made a superb model. I wasn't too young to start; by the time I was twenty-one I would be established in a respected and well-paid profession. If they felt, however, that I was too young, but later I decided on the career myself when I was old enough to choose, I should bear him in mind.

It was very interesting, but concerned the remote girl in the photographs, not me, especially when the Frightful Five had a roller-skating date in the big outdoor rink in Memorial Park.

Afterwards we shared two large pizzas at a table under the trees. Mandy said suddenly, "*Are* you going to be a model, April?"

My mouth was too full for me to even say "Huh?" Kim said it.

"You should see the pictures of her my cousin took at the class picnic," Mandy said. "We got a set today. My gosh, she looks like a high-fashion model."

"Kate's the beauty," I said through cheese and crumbs.

Mandy's sharp face was generous and enthusiastic. There was no malice in the bright eyes behind her big glasses. "He told my mother you'd be terrific. You could start doing kids' clothes now, and —"

"Would you be on TV commercials?" Kim demanded. "Magazine covers? In movies?"

"Everything!" Mandy breathed.

"I wouldn't want to be one," Teresa said. "They have to starve themselves. I could never give up food for my art."

"Neither could I," I said. "Mandy, you could be one because you'll never put on an ounce."

"I'm never even going to have a *figure*," she mourned.

"That's what they like!" I encouraged her.

"I'm not beautiful."

"You've got good bones," I said professionally.

"Well, this here gorgeous skeleton is going to be a politician," Mandy announced.

"And this one's going to be a lawyer," I said flatly, and took more pizza.

"But you *are* beautiful," Kim argued. "People look at you, I notice it all the time."

"Yes, what's it like?" Sheila asked me. They seemed fascinated and it made me self-conscious. I shrugged.

"I just don't think about it until somebody starts talking about it, like now. So let's not, huh? It makes me feel squirmy."

The rest laughed but Teresa said, "For your looks I wouldn't mind squirmy."

"You don't even have braces," said Sheila. Her mouthful of expensive hardware was a constant annoyance to her, and kept her from smiling pleasantly.

"Cheer up, you'll outgrow them," Mandy consoled her. "I have already. You'll be glad you went through it."

"That's what everybody says, but what a drag."

The talk was safely off me. . . . I knew people stared sometimes. If they smiled, I smiled back. I was never insolent, but I preferred not to notice that I was being looked at. It was a nuisance.

For the last two weeks of August my family and the Snows went to Nova Scotia and explored the whole beautiful province. My only disappointment was that Brendan couldn't go. He was driving a truck for a building-supply business.

Starting this fall he'd be a junior, and the year after next, he'd go away to Vermont to be a pre-med student. It could have been China as far as I was concerned. But I didn't dwell on it. In that wonderful summer the time of parting seemed light-years away.

90

Seventeen

That year I had a slumber party during Christmas vacation. When we were worn out enough to talk quietly from our sleeping bags, somebody brought up the Spring Festival. The senior high always had a winter carnival, with a king and queen, and the royalty had to be seniors. The junior high had its spring affair, with an elected princess who had to be an eighth-grader. On the Big Night the Winter King would lead her to be crowned by the Winter Queen.

We all thought Dodie Grossman would win the election. She was president of the class, an honor student, a good pianist always ready to help out, and with it all she was a genuinely good kid. She wasn't especially pretty, but popularity was important, and Dodie had it.

"Who'd dare to run against her?" some asked.

I said, "Phyllis." I had to say it, like swallowing a dose of bitter medicine and getting it over with. The others rose up in noisy surprise.

"Look at her objectively," I said. This word was one of my newest acquisitions, and sounded mature. "She'd have all the Fizz Ed crowd behind her. And can't you see her on the front page of the *Gazette* with that great big smile?"

"Dodie might not want to run," Teresa said. "She's pretty busy."

"Then we'll nominate *you*," Mandy pointed a finger at me like a gun.

"Look, everybody knows Phyllis, but who knows me?"

"You'd be surprised how many know that you're the prettiest girl in the school."

"This is just a disguise. I'm really a frog." We all laughed at that, even Mandy. About then my mother knocked on the door and said, "I hate to be a spoilsport, but it's after two in the morning!"

I completely forgot about the slumber-party chatter until Mandy the Politician sprang a surprise on me.

"We're nominating you, April," Mandy told me briskly. "I'll manage your campaign, and I know just how to do it. I've already been working behind the scenes."

"In those smoke-filled rooms we keep hearing about?" I asked. "You've got to be kidding, Mandy."

"She's not." Kim's pointed face was all aglow. "Dodie's not running, just like Teresa said. But Phyllis *is*."

"And you've got to be named quick," Sheila chimed in, "because there can only be twelve candidates." The one with the most votes would be Princess and the next six would be maids-in-waiting, the last five would be out.

"Beside Phyllis, I won't stand a chance," I said. "She's practically the best girl athlete in the whole junior high. She wins glory for the school. What do *I* do?"

"You," said Mandy, "are only the most beautiful girl in the school, that's all. And if that isn't glory, what is?"

"You are, you know," Teresa said solemnly. "*Bella, bella,*" she said in Italian.

"I'd hate you for it," Kim said, "if you weren't such a good kid, and besides, I like being seen with you. You've got such class. It's like having a real diamond necklace, or a prestige sports car."

"Or a thoroughbred Arabian horse," suggested Sheila.

"Gee, thanks." I felt foolish, but I was pleased too. Who wouldn't be after being called "a good kid"? "I don't know whether to sparkle, make engine noises, or whinny."

But Mandy wasn't losing sight of her goal. "They know you exist, all right. They just have to be prodded in the right direction."

"They think I'm stuck-up."

"They'll just have to find out you aren't."

Her confidence and the others' eagerness were contagious, though I really couldn't see myself being elected Festival Princess by a couple of hundred people most of whom knew me only by sight. But Mandy was positive. After all, she'd had experience going through her father's campaigns.

And they all kept saying, "You wouldn't want to see Phyllis get it, would you?"

Eighteen

I wanted to use Mr. Latimer's photographs on the posters Kim and Teresa were making, but my parents said I couldn't use them without his permission. Besides, he was a professional photographer, and that would be unfair to the others.

Mandy groaned when I told her. "This is *war*! You don't worry about fair or unfair!"

But we had to make do with the pictures she took, posing me with the dogs. Sheila wanted me in a tutu, standing on my toes, but Mandy said ballet would turn the boys off. She said the picture of me with Rolfe the Doberman would really get them.

"They'll probably elect him by a landslide write-in vote," I said. The others laughed but Mandy frowned on foolishness. As my campaign manager she was nervous, quick-tempered, always darting here and there to talk urgently to someone. She was so sure of victory that I began thinking, *Maybe . . . What if? . . . Stranger things have happened. . . .*

Phyllis, always surrounded by her cohorts, gave me an icy blue stare if we met. Well, I had cohorts now, and my committee reported that Rolfe was impressing the boys.

"I *told* you Rolfe is going to be arm in arm with the King out there on the stage that night," I said. Everybody thought that was funny but Mandy, who said stonily, "It's a good thing I'm not letting you run your own campaign. You'd never get off the ground."

On the posters they put our lists of activities. Mine was short, compared to some of the others. Mandy said dolefully that it was too late in the year for me to join a lot of things. But when I started high school I'd better get into everything I could, in preparation for being the Winter Queen.

"If you're Spring Festival Princess and then Winter Queen, you're a shoo-in for all the queen contests that come along after that. You could end up being Miss Universe!"

Prudently I didn't repeat this alluring prospect to my parents.

I was sorry when it came time to vote. The campaign had been fun, even if Mandy had been so deadly serious and expected me to be the same. I loved all the attention, the kids wanting to be around me as kids had surrounded Phyllis ever since I first knew her. If I lost, would I be like Cinderella at the stroke of twelve? But Mandy was sure I'd win, and she knew about these things.

We had a special assembly to hear the results.

Phyllis! The name crashed into my midriff like a basketball slammed at me from close range. I went cold all over, and there was a terrible noise in my head. It wasn't a sign that I was about to faint; it was Phyllis's crowd stamping and whistling. Then the applause started, and with my stomach twisting I clapped and clapped till my hands hurt. All the while I was wishing I'd never let myself be talked into anything that involved Phyllis.

A jab in the ribs made me gasp. It was from Mandy. Scarlet-faced, she said ferociously, "What are you clapping for, you dummy?"

"Because I'm a good loser!" I replied, just as ferociously.

"Well, she's a dirty winner! She smeared you and don't you forget it! Telling everybody you think you're already some kind of princess, spoiled rotten, never did anything for the school the way she has —"

Phyllis was called up to the stage. Beside me Mandy was trying not to weep with rage and disappointment. "I put up a good hard fight," she choked. "*You* could have worked harder, but you wouldn't!"

That stopped me from wanting to cry. Thank goodness nobody but the winner was supposed to go up front now. She shook hands with Mr. Amory, smiling shyly. (She was about as shy as a shark.) Her golden fleece streamed down her back. I imagined that inside she was wild with triumph over me. As a good sport I should congratulate her when we got back to our room; but I was positive she'd laugh in my face.

Nineteen

I got through the morning all right, but I couldn't face the cafeteria at noon, with Phyllis's gang uproarious across the room, and mine looking glum or sick or mad. I skipped out before Mandy could grab me, and ran a block in the mild spring noon. Then I walked the rest of the way, trying to calm down before I reached home.

My mother, just sitting down to lunch, said at once, "Are you sick?"

"Nope. I just came home to tell you Rolfe didn't win."

"Good heavens! He'll never be able to hold up his head in this town again. Have some salad?"

"I'll fix it."

"Wash your hands first," she said automatically. "Who did get it?"

"Phyllis."

"*No!*" She was suitably astonished.

"Well, why not?" I demanded. "She's always doing something or other that's supposed to be great for the school." I groaned. "And I have to be a maid-in-waiting for her. It'll kill me, I know it will. I'm going to drop out, and one of the tail-enders can take my place."

"Then you'll be *very* well known in school as a sore loser." She was sympathetic but firm. "No, April, you won't drop out. You'll stand up there with a pleasant expression on your face so your father and I can be proud of you. Now eat your lunch, and I'll drive you back to school."

"Yes, Mother," I said. There was a certain relief in having no choice. But I walked back, so nobody'd think I'd fled to Mom for comfort.

The coronation was five nights away. We six would come in from opposite sides of the stage, three to a side, to stately music; we'd wear long dresses and wreaths of spring flowers on our hair, and would carry bouquets. When we were in our places, the Winter Queen and her little page would enter and arrange themselves picturesquely by the footlights. The page would carry the crown on a cushion.

Then there'd be a mighty trumpet flourish, the curtains at the back of the stage would part, and reveal the Winter King and the Spring Princess in all their splendor. He would lead her forward and the Queen would set the delicate little crown on her head. Until the last rehearsal, the crown was a strip of cardboard held together with paper clips, and the girls' Fizz Ed teacher stood in for the Queen; the guidance counselor was King. Miss Torrance of the Drama Club directed.

Phyllis was all smiles at the rehearsals. The other runners-up, who'd known they hadn't a chance anyway, were perfectly happy to be part of the show, and I acted as if I felt the same way. It got easier and easier, especially after I caught Phyllis giving me sidewise looks as if she couldn't figure me out; I was supposed to be *crushed*, trying to smile bravely through unshed tears. But I was too busy showing the other maids-in-waiting that I was a good kid, and they were friendly when they realized I wasn't going to act like a spoiled brat who was furious at not winning.

On the great night we maids clustered together admiring each others' dresses. We'd been given our bouquets of spring flowers, courtesy of the P.T.A. Real, fragrant flowers, though the wreathes on our heads were artificial. In spite of the way I felt about Phyllis, the time had the joyous anxiety of the last moments before the curtain rose on one of our plays or a dance recital.

Mrs. Clements came in with Phyllis and kept fussing around her, touching up her hair with a brush, twitching at her white dress. Phyllis was like a puppet strung on wires, she couldn't stand still.

Finally we could hear the orchestra tuning up. Miss Torrance announced we had ten minutes to go. Mrs. Clements kissed Phyllis on the forehead, and said loudly, "Darling, we're so *proud* of you!"

She almost collided with Mandy in the doorway. Mandy shot toward me, out of breath, her cheeks red. Ignoring the others close to me she said, "I have to tell you something."

"Mandy, you shouldn't be here," Miss Torrance said. "April, Heather, Carrie, go along now to the other side, and be sure to wait for your cue."

We three, in green, peach, and yellow, went up the steps to the stage and past Bobby Saxon waiting to pull the curtain on this side. He was all one huge grin. This set off giggles in us which we frantically stifled as we crossed the stage. Thank goodness the orchestra was now playing Somebody-or-other's Spring Song.

Tim Wales was manning the curtain on the other side, and he was no more help than Bobby. But the sight of Miss Torrance in the wings opposite us was wonderfully sobering. The other three maids wore pink, blue, and lilac.

The overture finished. Outside the curtains Mr. Amory welcomed guests and described the special events of the next few days. Then a mighty chord on the piano instructed Bobby and Tim to haul with all their strength.

Miss Torrance cued us, and to somebody else's Spring Song we walked to our places. I was first in our group, so I stood close to the spot where Phyllis would shortly appear.

Now came the Winter Queen in her robes. She and the page looked as if they were in church. Down front the two trumpeters arose, and my stomach knotted in anxiety for them. How awful to mess it up in front of all those people, including their parents!

They did it, and got a big round of applause. Behind us, the back curtains parted and there stood Phyllis and the Winter King. He was a tall slim redhead, and in his white outfit he was as handsome as anybody I'd ever seen. Phyllis's hand rested on his arm.

She looked smashing. Her fair hair shimmered under the lights as if it had golden threads in it, and her skin glowed against white organza ruffles. I didn't resent Phyllis then; this moment was for the glory of the whole school.

Applause burst out, and the two walked slowly forward. The little crown sparkled on its cushion as if it were made of real gems. The applause went on and on, and the Winter King smiled like genuine royalty about to wave to his subjects. Phyllis's chin was up, and she was trying to look haughty, but failed because she was so pleased with herself. Well, I didn't blame her.

And then there was something else besides applause. At first I couldn't believe it, until I saw Mr. Amory's expression change from pleasure to anger as he swung around and looked out over the auditorium. Alarm struck at my sensitive stomach. I saw Phyllis's hand clamp hard on the King's arm, and his smile fading. In the opposite wings Miss Torrance pressed two fingers against her mouth.

Twenty

Loud boos were roaring through the applause. Spreading. Starting up in one place, and then, as people angrily turned around, stopping, and flaring up somewhere else. Phyllis was trembling, she looked absolutely terrified as she gripped the King's arm, and he'd lost his easy smile.

Adult voices were protesting, other kids were yelling, "Stop it! Shut up! Knock it off!" But it kept swelling up here and there. Mr. Amory had gone down onto the main floor, and the men teachers were walking up and down the aisles.

Suddenly the boos stopped. The applause took over with new strength as if to reassure Phyllis and the Winter King.

Mr. Amory came back, and made a little speech. "I apologize for the people who tried to ruin a beautiful and traditional occasion. But they can't do it if we don't let them. I will deal with them tomorrow. Now let us go on."

More loud applause and no more boos and catcalls. But on the stage we were still shaking, including Phyllis.

When she was crowned, the King led her to the three thrones, large chairs draped in damask portieres. Then each of the maids was introduced, in the order of their votes. The audience was impartial and gave everybody a good hand. Phyllis clapped too, and I admired the way she held together after such a terrible experience.

I smiled at the audience when my name was read out. *Well!* I got more than a good hand. I got earsplitting whistles. Cheers. Stamping. Yells. Such enthusiasm was so unexpected I forgot to smile. I could only stare, thinking, If so many people are that crazy about me, why wasn't I voted Princess?

It was as loud as the bad sound had been, and suddenly I had a horrid conviction that the two happenings were related. In delayed reaction I began to blush, I blushed all over, I was sweating under my dress and clutching my flowers hard enough to strangle them. Mr. Amory had to signal for silence. I wished I could fade backwards through the opening in the curtain, but if Phyllis could tough it out, so could I. I clenched my teeth to keep my jaw steady. Distantly I heard the applause for the last two girls. What I heard in my head was Mandy saying, "I have to tell you something!"

We had to sit three on each side of Royalty while the concert went on. It was the longest two hours of my life. We didn't dare whisper to each other, and I sat rigidly still, smiling at the right places, clapping when everybody else did, and all the time wondering what people were thinking of me.

On the surface, it sounded as if a lot of kids thought I should have won, and were making it clear. But I couldn't take any satisfaction out of it. If I'd won and Phyllis's crowd had put on such an ugly display, I don't know how I could have endured it. Besides that, it had spoiled the whole evening for a lot of people, not just Phyllis.

Mandy! Just wait until I get my hands on her.

Phyllis must have been thinking the same thing about me. At the concert's end we all stood to sing our school song, the band played, the applause was enormous, the curtains came together, and I turned to get off the stage as fast as I could without trampling anybody to death in the process. But Phyllis grabbed my wrist in a grip of steel and twisted it so I had to face her; my slightest movement caused me pain.

I can't tell you what she called me. You can fill in the blanks.

"Hey, cool it!" the King warned her, jerking his head toward the curtain. The other girls gathered around, and Bobby and Tim rushed over.

"Phyllis, please," I gasped. "I didn't — honestly, I didn't — " Outside the curtain, there was the uproar of people leaving and talking, and close by it Mr. Amory was heard discussing events with other teachers and members of the school board. One of the other maids said, "Phyllis, you *don't* know —"

"I know she's always been a dirty little liar," Phyllis said. "Ever since I first knew her. She thought she'd walk away with this because she's so *beautiful*" — she snarled the word — "and when she found out everybody wasn't crazy enough to bow down and worship her, she couldn't stand it. So she had to wreck it for me. For the whole school!" she added in a blaze of patriotic fervor.

The King muttered to the Queen, and they left rapidly, and no doubt thankfully, though the page looked wistfully back. Miss Torrance bore down on us. "Girls, what's going on here?"

Phyllis had to let me go. She strode out past the teacher. I let the others leave first, and just managed not to rub my burning, throbbing wrist.

I hurried out to our car. The evening was cool and I'd been sweating. Shivering in the car, I said aloud, "I hope I get pneumonia before morning."

My parents found me there about ten minutes later. My chivalrous father took off his blazer and put it around me, and I sat cozily between them on the ride home. They hadn't for a moment believed that I'd organized the demonstration, and I didn't name Mandy. Let them guess it for themselves. Well, there was no chance whatever that I'd ever run for princess or queen or class officer or anything. I was retiring from public life as of now.

At home I took a warm shower, then came downstairs in my robe and slippers to have hot tea and cinnamon toast with my parents. After I'd made a good start on the tea and toast we discussed what should be done. They'd guessed Mandy, of course, but I kept saying I didn't know, she'd never told me anything. Thank heavens, Miss Torrance hadn't given her the chance.

Twenty-one

Going to school the next morning was like walking to the guillotine. I was dressed for the execution in my leaf-green blazer and pleated skirt with a yellow and white checked shirt. When my homeroom teacher told me to report to the principal's office, that was the moment when they hoist up the blade and tell you to kneel. Her pat on my shoulder only weakened my knees all the more.

"I know you couldn't have been part of a conspiracy, April," she told me. How do you know? I wanted to ask her as I'd done in the third grade. If I were plain, or really ugly, would you still believe I'm innocent?

I doubted it. Her kindness was only the other side of the coin that showed resentment, jealousy, or hatred.

It's not fair, it's not fair! I always used to be yelling that, until Brendan stopped me. But it *wasn't* fair. There'd been no reason why I shouldn't try out for Princess. I tried, I lost, and that should have been the end of it. Instead, I was disgraced.

The others were already in Mr. Amory's office, Phyllis, in fighting trim, Mandy, pale and white-lipped. The other maids knew they were safe no matter what happened to the rest of us, and they'd have the delight of telling everybody else What Happened.

Phyllis, as the injured party, got to tell her story first.

"She had it all fixed up with Mandy," she said. "I heard them. Mandy came into the shower room and said, 'I've got everything fixed,' and they went into a corner, and they were *laughing.*"

She glared at me.

She was so convincing I kept trying to remember how it really was.

"April?" Mr. Amory said.

"Mandy came in," I said slowly. "But we didn't talk. Did we, Mandy?"

I knew Mandy was calculating whether or not to haul me into it. I wanted to defend myself, but I didn't want to be disloyal to her.

Heather spoke up. "Mandy came in but they didn't talk, Mr. Amory. It was time to begin. We had to hurry."

Carrie and another of the maids confirmed this. Phyllis sputtered, "But she *did* know! She can't stand it because she lost! Everything's supposed to go her way! And she's always hated me!"

"That's enough, Phyllis," Mr. Amory said.

I took advantage of being safe in a crowd, and plunged. "Phyllis, you wouldn't let me apologize before, but I'm sorry for what happened."

"Oh, yeah?" said Phyllis nastily.

"Phyllis, that's no way to accept an apology," said Mr. Amory.

"Who says I'm accepting?"

"Perhaps you'd better think twice about that, Phyllis. You told a false story about what happened in the shower room, but I don't hear April demanding an apology from you."

Phyllis went even redder. She set her square jaw and stared out the window.

"Phyllis, you may go back to your room, and the rest of you go too, except April and Mandy."

Phyllis marched out. The maids scurried like a batch of partridge chicks.

"April," Mr. Amory said, "can you give me your word that you knew nothing about this demonstration?"

"Yes." But I didn't want to sound like Goody Two-shoes. "Only I know why — I mean, *I* didn't care so much that I didn't win, but Mandy worked so hard —" I was falling all over myself.

"We should have won!" Mandy cried. "It wasn't fair!" (I heard myself in that.)

"How'd you arrange the demonstration, Mandy?" he asked her. "Did you pay the others? Promise them anything?"

"No," she said proudly. "I got the kids who think the Festival's stupid and baby stuff. And there were some boys who wanted to give Pete a hard time." Pete was the Winter King.

"It's politics!" she flung defiantly at the principal. "Everything's fair in politics!"

"Maybe you think so, Mandy," he said, "but it's not the way we run the Spring Festival. Would you care to name these students? We picked out a few of them on the scene last night. So if we're talking about fairness, why shouldn't they all be in on this?"

"Can I go?" I asked from a scrapy dry throat.

"Yes, and ask Miss Holstrom to come in with her notebook, please."

Mandy stared out the window, as Phyllis had. I spoke to the secretary in the outer office and took sanctuary in the girls' room where I fought off my own tears.

It was a successful battle and I took comfort from that as I collected my books and went to my first class. Mandy came a while later. She never looked at me all morning.

I wasn't going to run home like that third-grader way back. I was going to eat my lunch and to heck with everybody else. I shot out a side door the first chance at the corner where my campaign committee had always met. If they wanted to join me, okay. Otherwise, I'd have it all to myself.

I then realized I was fair game for Phyllis, but she stayed a good distance away from me, surrounded by her cohorts. It was Mandy who nailed me. She came with Kim and Teresa. Sheila was missing. I found out why later.

"What did you apologize for?" Mandy demanded. "I thought you hated her! You went and spoiled everything by being so smarmy! I almost threw up!"

"Spoiled what?" I demanded right back. "You already did that, with your stupid idea!"

"You should've won. I worked hard enough for it. And if you didn't, at least we could make her good and miserable. But you had to go and crawl to her. *Yuck!*"

"I didn't crawl! If anybody did to me what you did to her, I'd have been ready to kill 'em. You messed up something for the whole school, not just something for her."

"I did it for you, and this is all the thanks I get."

"I thank you for trying to get me elected, but not for creating a disturbance at the concert."

"Creating a disturbance!" she mimicked. "*La*-di-*da!* Well, thank you for nothing. I'll never work for you or even *speak* to you again." She tramped off, her faithful crew behind her, and I shouted after her, "Is that a threat or a promise?"

Mandy and her eighteen helpers got detention for two weeks, and had to apologize to Phyllis. Kim was one of the girls, but Teresa had been playing in the orchestra the whole time. Sheila had chickened out at the last minute. After the lights went out she'd left her post and sat next to the school librarian, who could thus vouch for her later.

114

So Mandy had dropped her with a loud crash.

Kim and Mandy now turned their heads away from me when I was near, as if I smelled bad. Teresa did too.

"Never mind," Brendan said to me. "With them for friends, who needs an enemy?"

"I don't mind," I said. "At least I don't think I do. I mean I don't miss *them*, but I miss something. I don't know what."

"I hope you haven't stopped speaking to all the kids you tried to charm into voting for you."

"Of course not," I said indignantly.

"And do they say Hi back?"

"Yup. Why?"

"There you are. There ought to be some friends somewhere in the bunch."

"You and Claire and Kathleen are my friends, that's all. And the dogs."

This was on my thirteenth birthday.

Twenty-two

While we rehearsed for our ballet recital, Sheila told me how she'd tried to talk Mandy out of her wild idea, and Mandy told her she had no killer instinct.

"Join the club," I said.

Sheila was all right, but I missed the fun we'd all had together, when we'd sparked one another into wit and laughter and adventure. I was rather relieved when Sheila went out West to spend the summer with relatives.

I sewed for myself, attended to my clients, and grandmother-sat once a week.

Matt still happened to be there when I was. It was a funny thing about New Boy. Whenever we passed each other in the school corridors or on the street, it was with barely a nod. At the most, there was a quick "Hi." But when we met at the Andrews' house it was as if last summer were still going on. There were the card games, the lazy sipping and listening while Mrs. Chisholm remembered her way through a life that, I used to think enviously, was a lot more exciting than anything I'd ever have.

Sometimes she fell suddenly asleep, and

without any effort Matt and I would talk. Our conversations wandered in the most unusual directions. They were never about school, and I appreciated that, after the Spring Festival mess.

There were things about which Matt knew a great deal. Yet, whenever we met away from that house, his narrow dark face was quiet and secret, as if never in his life had he told about Viking voyages, Mayan temples, and dinosaurs in western canyons.

Phyllis was away in camp, of course. Mrs. Clements didn't speak to my mother. Mandy, Kim, and Teresa didn't speak to *me*. Whenever I tried to unravel this tangled mess, I became more confused. What had I done? Whenever I looked at that mysterious stranger in my mirror I would think, You're as much a misfit in your way as the kids Dodie Grossman always goes out of her way to be nice to.

So I resolved that I'd go out of my way for them too in the future.

There was fun at the farm, but not as often as when we were all small. Brendan was with us occasionally on his day off, but he had friends of his own age — boys *and* girls. I tried not to resent this. After all, Claire and Kathleen liked me, and a girl needs other girls to laugh and whisper with.

My parents and I went to Quebec on our vacation. That passed too quickly. I began waking in the night from disturbing dreams, and each dawn I would count the days until

I had to start school. My dread cast a horrible shadow over what should have been wonderful. Finally, the day after we got home, I told my mother.

"But you won't be going to the same school," she said. "It'll be high school now. Aren't you thrilled at that? I was."

"No," I said morosely. "Because I'll be going with the same old kids. In fact I've been in school with the same old kids since the Year One. I'm sick of their faces, and I know darn well they're sick of mine."

"Well, April," she said, "school is a fact of life and I think you'll have to accept it."

"They have freshman record hops," I gloomed. "Everybody just comes to the gym on the night, and they're supposed to mix. What if you go and nobody asks you to dance?"

"How do you know that'll happen to you?"

"Because I don't know any boy that likes me."

"I'm sure some of them do," she said, "but they're too bashful to show it. Just the way you must feel about some of them."

I did, but I wouldn't admit it. If any one of those splendidly confident creatures whom I admired should ask me to dance, I'd had gone numb and speechless.

"What about Matt?" asked my mother.

I laughed loudly. "*Him*? He wouldn't be caught dead at a dance! And I'm not going, either. And I'm not going to parties or *giving* any. Slumber or otherwise."

"All right, dear," said my mother. "When are you supposed to be at the Marshalls' to hold the cat while he gets his eardrops?"

"I'm going right now," I said. I took off on my bike, a little deflated because I hadn't run into opposition to my ultimatum. It also made me suspicious.

Twenty-three

The only thing I signed up for in school was The Thespians. I'd have a substantial study load, my clients took a lot of my time, and I was having an extra hour of advanced ballet each week.

I knew I wouldn't get much to do in Thespians as a freshman — no acting parts this year unless it was in a crowd scene. We would read plays, study them, and go to Community Theatre performances in our town and neighboring ones, and to professional events in the city. As in junior high, Pam didn't join; she went to Saturday classes at a dramatic academy in Bixby.

Mr. Hamilton announced that we would be attending a performance of *The Merchant of Venice* in Bixby in October. We were to read the play aloud first so we'd understand the Elizabethan speech. I didn't expect to do anything but listen to the readings, so I was surprised when Mr. Hamilton, a stout man with many chins, shone upon me one day like the rising sun.

"April, I hear you plan to become a lawyer. So you'll come to our next meeting prepared to read Portia in the courtroom scene."

I was overcome. Some of the senior girls must have been looking forward to that scene, and I didn't want to start off on the wrong foot with all these older kids.

But I'd do the best I could. Mr. Hamilton didn't expect acting, just clearness of diction, respect for punctuation, and an ear for rhythm.

I looked up the scene as soon as I got home, and this was my introduction to the famous "quality of mercy" speech. I thought it was beautiful. I read it again and again, walking back and forth in my room with the book in my hand, and watching my reflection. I was passionate, or quietly intense, or very gentle, which I thought was the most impressive. I tried the readings out on my parents, and asked their opinion.

My father said he hoped I'd adopt a medium course when I was actually a trial lawyer. The jury wanted neither to be ranted at nor whispered to. My mother said she couldn't decide which reading she liked best, and wasn't it too bad American lawyers didn't wear robes in court?

What I hadn't thought about was that I would be standing up in a roomful of people, reading the part with BOYS. *Older* ones. It rather shook my confidence, though I'd knotted my hair on my neck that day to make me look more mature, and I knew I looked well enough in a favorite dark blue skirt and vest over a pink plaid shirt.

But help came from the other readers.

Reid Bennett, the senior who did Shylock that day, was a shaggy, rather nondescript boy until he began to read. He had his own ideas about Shylock. On our first exchange I felt the hair standing up on the back of my neck. This was like nothing else I'd ever known. This was *It*!

The bright classroom, the others standing around with their books or watching from their seats, Mr. Hamilton leaning against the wall at one side — everything else faded to mist beyond a glass wall.

I followed my father's advice and took a middle course for the "mercy" speech. I knew I did it well. Portia was mine; I was Portia.

Some of the other voices were young and awkward — I suppose mine was the same, in spite of my passion for the part — but Reid stood out. It was a lovely, exhilarating experience to be slashing our speeches back and forth at each other, and when he left the scene, dignified in defeat, the life went out of it for me. But I did my best to the end. I had some more good speeches, even though Antonio and Bassanio, a sophomore and a junior, didn't seem as grown-up as I felt.

We finished, and were applauded by every one. I was glad to sit down. My legs felt weak, I was sweating. "Nice going, Portia!" Reid Bennett said, patting my shoulder.

After that he called me Portia if we met in the corridors. I was proud and embarrassed, and felt so foolish because I couldn't do anything but grin. *Where's your poise, you nut?* I scolded myself.

How could I have ever thought Reid was nondescript? His thick dark hair was rough, he didn't much care what he wore — though he was clean enough — but his deepset dark eyes had a grown-up sparkle. And what a voice he had, when he chose to use it! He wasn't at all self-conscious about putting everything into a part, whether it was comedy or tragedy. There were other good actors in Thespians, but I thought he was the best.

In fact I thought so much about Reid Bennett that my tragedy for this year was knowing he'd be graduated and long gone by the time I could have had a date with him.

The professional performance in Bixby was magnificent, with all the costumes and the settings, but I still thought that Reid Bennett's Shylock was the best. Some day he'd be as famous as Sir Laurence Olivier.

And by then, I dreamed away while dog-walking, the difference in our ages wouldn't really *be* a difference.

Twenty-four

With my fourteenth birthday at the end of April, the school year was almost over, and it had gone by in the twinkling of an eye, as the fairy tales say. Three years of hard work lay between me and the awesome Mt. Everest of college and law school. What was important right now was that real dates lay only two years away. In between were the minor ones, going on bike rides or to the movies with a boy, to parties or small dances, even if somebody's father drove you there and brought you home.

And I was going to wake up some morning miraculously knowing how to talk to BOYS. Or to listen, which my mother told me was important too. But you had to have one around to listen *to*.

Reid Bennett graduated. He wasn't to be an actor, he planned to study business administration. I was disillusioned.

Brendan graduated from St. Patrick's High and we were all there. He would go to the University of Vermont in September, and it seemed like halfway around the world to me. Supposing he had the time to talk, my toll calls would eat up my allowance. Besides, his girl was going there too, so he'd never think of calling *me*. I loathed her secretly, because Claire and Kathleen were crazy about her.

During my fourteenth summer Matt still showed up to do his work when I was with old Mrs. Chisholm. He was always annoyingly the same; he didn't even seem to grow.

Once I stopped and watched him clipping grass along the walk. He clicked away like a machine, never noticing me. Finally I snapped at him, "Is that all you ever do? Just mosey around from day to night? Are you going to go moseying through your whole life?"

After an exasperating pause he replied, slowly, "I might."

I felt like kicking him. I was very cross because my life was fleeting by without any romance or drama. I was even tired of reading romantic poetry and dreaming about a theatrical career as Reid Bennett's leading lady, especially since he wasn't going to replace Sir Laurence Olivier.

I was further enraged when Matt came up on the porch and drank at least half the iced tea.

"I don't know what I'll do when you two are off in college, living exciting lives," Mrs. Chisholm said. Matt went on munching chocolate chip cookies.

"I won't forget you, Mrs. Chisholm," I said.

"You will when the boys come flocking around."

I looked sidewise at Matt, daring him to smirk or at least lift an eyebrow, but he was too busy refueling. Mrs. Chisholm went on talking happily about her school days. I gloomed. I didn't want to wait until college for the flock to arrive. One or two right now would constitute a flock for my purposes. My mother was always telling me boys my age were shy but, having seen them in action, I doubted it. No, it was *me*. Maybe I was beautiful, but not to them.

The Thespians planned a big Christmas play, and then in the spring they were going to do *You Can't Take It with You*, and join with the Glee Club in *The Pirates of Penzance*. There'd be plenty of jobs for everybody, on stage and off.

If you had the points you could graduate at the end of your junior year, and this appealed to me. I didn't discuss it with my parents but took on more work. After all, I had the time. I only wished I were a genius who could finish high school right now.

I saw Brendan alone for a few minutes when we were skiing through the woods on Christmas Day.

"How are things, Ape?" he asked kindly.

"Oh, fine." I was breezy. "I'm graduating at the end of my junior year. That's what I'm concentrating on now."

"Any boys around?"

"Are you *kidding*?" I burst out. "They stay away in *crowds*!" I forgot my resentment of Brendan's girl. After all, Brendan always

126

understood my panic, even if he scolded me for it. "Some girls can just say hello to a boy when she goes by him, and he'll catch up with her. If I say hello, what happens next? *Nothing!* I feel like such a dope!"

He had an odd little smile. Finally he said, "You're young yet. You'll learn."

It was an easy way out for him, now that he had a girl who presumably knew how to talk to boys. In the old days we'd have kept on arguing until something finally came clear, but all I got now was this little smile and shake of the head.

Twenty-five

I'd have ignored the Winter Carnival, but my parents made a big thing out of attending some of the events. I suspected it was for my good. I couldn't refuse to go, but I wasn't very gracious. There was something shameful about being with your parents instead of with at least one friend, if not a crowd.

While we were watching the figure skating one afternoon, my mother said in my ear, "There's a boy trying to catch your eye. Why don't you speak to him and put him out of his misery?"

In hope I turned my head quickly. But I saw, with a horrible depressed slumping in my stomach, that it was only Jason Barrett, referred to in Thespians as The Gopher, because he ran his short legs off for everybody.

"Oh, hi, Jase," I said distantly.

He turned so hotly scarlet that his glasses steamed. "Hi, April!" He rushed right over and I had to introduce him.

He shook hands with both my parents, and acted as if meeting them was what he'd been waiting for all his life. They responded to his enthusiasm and good manners. I tried not to look as sour as I felt, and hoped that everyone else was paying strict attention to the skaters.

"Can I get you some roasted chestnuts?" Jason was earnestly asking. "W-warms your hands."

"Oh yes, sure! Great idea!" My father reached for his billfold.

"No, sir, it's my treat," Jason said. He glanced at me and turned crimson again. My mother said quickly, "Go along with him, April."

Oh well, back to the old guillotine. In height he came about to my ear and sort of lunged along, hands in pockets and head pushed forward. Thank heavens Phyllis and her cohorts were nowhere in sight between us and the chestnut roaster. A bunch of little kids noisily surrounded it, and the two senior boys in charge were too busy to notice us beyond taking Jason's money.

We came away each carrying two hot little paper bags. Once free of the children we were all alone in an open space, and Jason stopped short and turned to face me. "I've been trying to get my nerve up for a couple of weeks to ask you something." His voice cracked and he cleared his throat. "It's now or never."

Make it never, I thought, but from personal experience I knew desperation when I saw it and couldn't help pitying him. "What is it?" I asked.

"Will you go to the ice party with me tonight?"

I stared at him thinking, *What a nerve! Imagine being seen out on a date with him!* But he was staring back at me with his brown eyes swimming behind his glasses, like Jones's when he didn't want to be left behind. . . . And I thought, *Okay, so he's an oddball but so am I. What if anybody laughs? I ought to be used to it by now.*

He lost his courage. "Forget it. You probably have a date already."

"'I don't have a date," I said. "Sure, I'll go with you, Jase. I'd love to."

He was speechless. Then his astonishment gave way to a grin of such pure blinding delight that it made me laugh.

"Oh my gosh," he breathed. Then he thrust his packages of chestnuts at me. "Here, take these. I can't stand around and talk now, I'll blow up or something." He started away, then came back. "I'll call for you around seven. Okay if we walk?"

"Sure. Thanks for the chestnuts!" He waved and left in a headlong rush. I was relieved not to have him around while I tried to think up ways to get out of going. But I knew I couldn't cold-bloodedly do that to him.

Of course my mother expected me to put on the skating outfit she'd made for me and which so far I'd worn only out on the farm pond at the Snows'. It was jade green wool, the skirt lined with pale yellow, and there were warm wool tights to match. And a knitted yellow cap and scarf and mittens. I hated dressing up as if it were a real date, and I hated the way she and my father pretended it was. But — as always — I was expected to put a good face on things and mind my manners. Handsome is as Handsome does.

When Jason came, he looked at me as if he couldn't believe his eyes, and I swear his glasses steamed up again. I just kept praying that nobody would notice us. I didn't have much faith though. I felt about as inconspicuous as the Statue of Liberty. If only he were *taller*, I thought, that'd be *something*.

The evening was beautiful, with the still dry cold that seems hardly cold at all. Surprisingly, he was a fine skater, so I could enjoy my own skating without being embarrassed by his.

The full moon appeared rose-gold over Orr's Hill, and we went round and round to the music of Strauss waltzes. It was all so beautiful I was glad I'd come, and gliding hand in hand with Jason seemed perfectly natural. On the ice he was a totally different creature from that blushing, plunging boy on land.

Everyone looked happy. We were all in a crystal spell of moonlight, music, and motion. Only once did something threaten to shatter it, when we came face to face with Phyllis and Bobby Saxon.

"Oh look!" Phyllis cried merrily. "April's brought her teddy bear!"

"Who's that with you?" I said. "Old Grizzly?"

Bobby thought that was funny. "So long, guys!" he called, still laughing as Phyllis towed him away.

"I'm sorry," I said to Jason, who had a quiet, stunned expression. "Phyllis is like that. You have to ignore her." Some advice coming from *me*.

"Do you want to go home now?" he asked.

"Why, for heaven's sake?"

"Maybe you're embarrassed, being with me."

"I'm not embarrassed." Strangely, this was true. "Mad, maybe. But I've been mad with Phyllis since the third grade. I'm used to it. It keeps me toned up."

He was trying to grin. "Gets the old adrenalin going, huh?"

"Yup. Come on. Stand by while I try a spin. I'm likely to land on my nose."

I had to be home by ten. We walked back along quiet streets, talking easily like old friends, stopping to pick out stars past the bare maple branches. When we reached the house my parents were upstairs, reading in bed, and there was a snack for us in the kitchen: hot chocolate and egg sandwiches, my favorite.

Jason was happy enough at the start, but soon became nervous. He kept staring at me and I kept trying to keep up the conversation, but I had to give up. "What's the matter?"

"I just want to thank you for one of the best nights of my life!" His voice betrayed him again. "You're so darn nice — you're nothing like what they said!" He grabbed his mug and gulped hot chocolate as if it were something stronger and he needed it.

"Who said *what*?" I asked with great poise. "Come on, Jase. Somebody said I was stuck-up, didn't they? Wouldn't give you the time of day."

"They dared me to ask you. See, there's this club, and I can be in it if I take a dare. Well, I thought it was going to be something simple, like walking a tightrope across Moosewood Falls." His mouth twitched. "Not ask the most beautiful girl in the school for a date."

"Did they say you had to *get* the date to be accepted into their stupid club?"

"Well, see, that'd be the only proof I asked."

"Well, I'm glad I helped out, then. Have some more hot chocolate."

"No, listen, April," he said desperately. "*Stupid* is the right word. It was so darn important to me once. I thought it would make me feel like one of the macho guys, not just somebody born to be everybody's gopher. But how in heck can I believe they're anything so special when I know they're so wrong? They say you think you're so far above everybody else you don't even see us. You're the Ice Maiden, or a —"

"A cold fish?" I supplied helpfully.

"Well, you aren't. You took on Old Short 'n' Shaggy, and you didn't care, and I had the best evening of my life, except for the time I got my dog. And oh yes," he added meticulously, "my ten-speed bike. And when we found out my father wasn't going to die after a bad accident."

"I know how I love *my* father — and my Jones" — my eyes prickled with tears — "and *my* bike. So if you class me with your father and your dog and your bike, I'm honored."

"You mean that, don't you?" he said in wonder.

"Yes, I do, Old Short 'n' Shaggy." I filled up our mugs again. "I'm starved. You know what? You're a good skater. Did you ever try out for hockey?"

"Yeah, but whenever there was a pile-up I was at the bottom. They clobbered me. I'm a born victim."

"You don't have to be, any more than you have to be everybody's gopher. And that so-called macho club wouldn't have done anything for you either. You have to do it yourself."

"That's easy for you to say. Look at you. Everything must just fall into your lap."

"Hah!" I said scornfully. "My looks have been my handicap since the third grade. Anything I get, brother, I'll get by hard work. Speaking of that, if you're really crazy about the theater, couldn't you work up to a career in it? Staging, set design, stage manager, stuff like that?"

"Because I could never be an actor, is that it?"

"Not acting?" he asked quickly. "I didn't know you were interested in the acting part."

"Any part of it I love," he said fervently. "But Mr. Hamilton did tell me I was a good property man."

"Then forget that bunch of numbskulls and just concentrate on what *you* want."

"Maybe you're right. You know, the joke's on them. I don't think they'd let me into their club anyway, they were just setting me up to make a fool out of me. But it didn't turn out that way after all."

"Because we're both your basic nice persons," I said, and we laughed. When he left we wished each other Happy New Year, even though it was February. But it seemed appropriate. I said I'd go skating with him again next Friday night if the ice was still good. While I was clearing up the dishes it dawned on me that I'd talked to him as Brendan used to talk to me.

Twenty-six

The next morning I was hanging my jacket up in my locker, when someone said loudly, "Too bad when the quote prettiest girl in the tenth grade unquote can't get any date but a little squirt nobody else would be caught dead with."

"Pathetic, isn't it?" said another voice.

Chuckles, and a third voice. "Shows that most people aren't fooled by looks."

The first speaker was Goldilocks Phyllis, female incarnation of Attila the Hun, with henchmen — henchpersons — at the ready. We were drawing a small but attentive audience.

"Gosh, Phyl, you demoted me. Last night I heard I was the most beautiful girl in the whole school."

"That must have thrilled you."

I shrugged. "Oh, I've got used to it since you first called it to my attention when we were about seven."

Color rushed up her neck into her cheeks. "How many men were in line ahead of your furry little friend?"

"I never bother to count. I just shut my eyes and point." Somebody behind Phyllis laughed. "I believe in sharing the wealth. One has a duty. They call it *noblesse oblige*." This got another laugh. Several. Phyllis slitted her eyes at me while she tried to think of a murderous reply. Bobby Saxon was approaching. "After all," I went on, "it doesn't do a person any harm to be seen with the most beautiful girl in the school, does it?"

I gave Bobby my sweetest smile, closed my locker, and walked away. "Did you hear *that*?" Phyllis demanded. "She's an egomaniac! She could be *dangerous*!"

"Who, *April*?" asked Bobby incredulously.

When I reached my homeroom I realized I'd left my books and notebooks in my locker. Never mind, my great exit was worth the return trip. Almost everybody was out of the corridor now, and before I got back to my locker the bell rang for morning exercises.

I'd have to wait a few minutes now, and in the enforced pause I knew that inside me I was shaking. Why does she hate me? I kept asking. When will she stop? I don't take anything from her, I don't compete with her. The one time I did, she won. So *why*?

I ought to be able to deal with her by now. I'd told Jason I could. But that was a lie.

I went into the girls' room and tried to talk to myself like Brendan, but it didn't work, mainly because Brendan, between his premed studies and his girl, probably wouldn't have the patience to listen. He'd make me feel emotionally immature for even mentioning it.

I looked dismally at my reflection. Phyllis and plenty of others behaved as if I'd stolen my looks from an innocent victim whom I'd left hunchbacked. But I couldn't help the way I was.

I was now determined to graduate at the end of my junior year. I talked to the guidance counselor after school that day, and he told me to discuss it with my parents.

I told them that night, after we'd had my father's favorite dessert, squash pie. It was supposed to put him in a mellow mood. What I got was one of those silent stares that speak volumes, as they say.

"But you're so busy now," my mother said, "how would you handle all the extra work? We want you to have some time to yourself. You're still growing, you need it."

"It's out of the question," my father announced. "Once you start college, you'll have a heavy workload for the next four years — eight, if you're still interested in the law. And for the next two years you'll have enough to do without trying to cram the two into one."

"I don't have to work that hard," I argued. "You know I can do the extra work with no sweat. I can hardly *wait* to get out of high school!"

"Why?" my mother asked.

"Because it's all so boring. I'll be glad to get to college where they'll be thinking about something serious, like getting down to your life's work."

"You can wait two years for college," my father said in that final tone.

Jason and I skated again a few nights later. It was fun, and when we ate afterwards we talked about our careers. He'd been getting advice from Mr. Hamilton, and he knew what colleges he should apply to, and what sort of practical experience he should try to get on the side.

Getting to know him this well, I forgot to worry about how much shorter he was, and I think he forgot it too. He was intelligent and had a sense of humor. He said that when the other boys asked him about his dates with me he just smiled mysteriously, and it was driving them all nuts.

Twenty-seven

The weatherman began talking about a soft spell coming, and Jason hunted me out in the cafeteria one noon and said, "Come on skating again tonight. It may be our last chance."

Because of other things going on in town, there weren't many people on the ice that night, just a few devoted skaters who wanted to get in all they could before the thaw. Jason and I went round and round in the moonlight, not talking, not touching, just enjoying the motion. I had no cares when I was on the ice, and in my jade green skating dress I felt like a *prima ballerina*, except that skating's easier on the toes. I was singing "Invitation to the Waltz" in my head when a tall stranger came gliding toward us and held out his hands to me; puzzled, I kept moving forwards, and he skated elegantly backwards, still holding out his hands. Laughing at the strangeness of it — and he was smiling too — I turned to Jason, and he was grinning, the light bright on his glasses. He took my hand and put it in the stranger's and said, "Go ahead, it's all right."

Like figures in a dream we went on, the

tall stranger and I, side by side now and holding hands. Jason was a little way off but abreast of us. Yes, it still felt like a dream when I turned my head to look at the stranger. He wore dark pants and sweater and a dark watch cap on the back of his very blond head. His hair was cut short, but a lock fell over his forehead.

I'd never seen him before that I could remember, and I had this weird, sad, half-frightening feeling that I'd never see him again. That we'd go floating over the ice like this to the end of the pond and then he'd disappear as mysteriously as he had appeared.

Well, we finished up neatly at the Snack Bar instead. It was Jason who had disappeared, and the Stranger Prince ordered two hot chocolates. Then he looked down at me and said, "Hello. I'm Nicholas, Nick, Barrett, Jase's brother."

"Hello." In my confusion I took a big drink, and gasped as hot marshmallow plastered my upper lip. Leave it to me! I tried to wipe it off with my tongue, feeling foolish.

"I wanted to meet you," Nick said gravely, "because you've been so nice to Jase."

I felt even more foolish. That darned marshmallow. Very seriously he handed me a paper napkin.

"Thank you. Jase is a good kid," I said.

"He's the best. But being short, and being Jase, he has a hard time. Only now I think he's coming out of it. He's thinking more of

141

himself and less of those creeps who've tried to make his life miserable. And it's all because of you."

"*Me!* Why?" I was startled enough to look directly at him. His eyes were a different blue from Brendan's. Lighter, like the sea on a summer day.

"Because a girl like you took the trouble to be nice to him. You could have set him back five years, but you didn't. The most beautiful girl in the school went on a date with him. Can't you see what that means? And then the way you talk to him — he told me — you've convinced him of his own worth. Something the rest of us couldn't do."

"Well," I said. I was blushing, shaky, and not just because of the compliments. "Jase has been a help to me too! If it wasn't for him I'd be skating alone here or not skating at all. Where is he, anyway?" I kept trying to locate the short figure. I didn't know if I liked the way Big Brother had simply taken over, as if Jason should humbly disappear on cue, and *I* should be thrilled.

Well, I was, but I'd be darned if I'd let *him* know.

Nick smiled. "You're like the girl in the old song; you're gonna dance with the guy what brung you. Jase is right over there talking to another girl, and it's all because you gave him the confidence to do it. Here they come."

Sure enough, Jason and a girl as short as himself were skating toward us. Jase was all one big grin. The girl was a chubby little thing I knew by sight. She seemed impressed by Nick and me, and this made me feel terribly adult. Jason ordered hot chocolate for Cindy and himself and said to her, "What were you saying about modern theater?" Cindy giggled, and Jason began telling her what *he* thought about modern theater.

"Why haven't I seen you before?" I asked Nick. "You don't go to school here, do you?"

"No, I go to John Paul Jones. This is our break after midyears." I knew about that hard-boiled prep school across the state.

"Are you going to Annapolis?" I asked respectfully.

"Yes, if I can get the appointment. I want that more than anything else on earth. I've loved the Navy all my life." He looked stern and mature. "If I don't get the appointment I'll join up and move up through the ranks."

"I hope you get your heart's desire," I heard myself saying.

"Thanks, April," he said. It was a solemn moment, and it was as if we two were alone on that frozen lake in the moonlight.

Nick was sixteen and could drive his father's car. We took Cindy home first, and then he and Jason came into my house with me. In the lamplight he was beautiful, I thought. (In a manly way, of course.) I just wanted to sit and look at him. I knew my parents liked him by the way they acted. And Jason was so proud of him, he kept beaming.

I had a hard time getting to sleep that

night. I went over and over the whole evening, and every time I reached the choice bit where he came skating up to me out of the moonlight, holding out his hands, it got better and better. And the next morning I knew even before I woke up that something wonderful had happened. If I'd ever thought I'd been in love before — I *knew* it this time.

My parents were so impressed by Nick's poise and dedication that the car rule was relaxed. I'm sure they thought he was simply transporting Jason and me around like a kindly older brother, and I thought so too, until the day the four of us went on a cross-country ski tour, and Nick and I got some distance ahead of Jase and Cindy. We were both longer-legged and speedier, so after a while we stopped to let them catch up with us.

After all my worry about talking with BOYS, here I was practically alone in the wilderness with one, and managing pretty well. I asked him questions about his school and about the Navy, and he answered and explained, gazing at me with those bright sea-blue eyes, his bare head yellow in the winter sunshine. I could just imagine him in uniform up on the bridge of a big vessel, looking out across a stormy ocean, responsible for the whole ship. Cold and calm.

One thing, he didn't have a line, he was too serious for that, and he didn't expect me to be witty. I couldn't have been to save my life. I was too overcome.

But a girl *knows*. She has a sixth sense — and dumb as I felt, I realized all at once that day that Nick wanted to be with me. Nothing was said, but the sweet certainty came to me and stayed.

One night we all went to the movies to see a big science fiction feature, and came out arguing vehemently about UFOs. We went to eat at The Wickiup later, and when we walked in past a booth crowded with Phyllis, Bobby Saxon, and some others, I felt as if there were a special personal radiance about Nick and me that nobody could miss. As if we were Enchanted People. Bobby yelled, "Hi, kids!" But Phyllis looked sulky and blank.

We went to our school's big hockey game with Cavendish High, and we won, and I was sad under all the glory because Nick would be going back across the state to John Paul Jones. Then, the next morning, he called up and asked if I'd like to take a walk in the country.

I didn't realize the other two wouldn't be with us until he showed up alone. He had a knapsack on his back, with plenty of lunch for the two of us, he said, but my mother insisted on adding brownies. Then we set off in a fine mild morning that promised spring even though the official date was weeks away. I guess I'd have felt like spring even in a snowstorm, if Nick was in it with me. We went a little way on the Cavendish road, then took off on a winding, narrow road I'd never been on before, and were soon in a landscape of farms and hardly any traffic.

We'd made only casual remarks about the weather and the scenery until we sat down on a boulder by the side of the road to rest and eat apples. "Where's Jase today?" I asked.

"Do you miss him?" He was staring steadily at the crows in a newly ploughed field.

"I just wondered, that's all," I said.

"He's helping Cindy with a history assignment. Are you disappointed because they didn't come?" Then he gave me that direct bright sea-blue look, and I could only be honest.

"Not really. It's just that I'm not a very good talker."

"You sound as if you're apologizing. Don't. Who needs talk? We can listen to the birds. Or the silence."

So it was all right, and we went on. Used to walking, I kept up with him easily. We went off on a lumbering road through deep woods, to a special place he had in mind for us to eat our lunch. It was in a clearing where we could sit on an old stone wall in the sunshine. A squirrel objected noisily to us, a woodpecker worked away on a dead tree, and there were chickadees.

We were being very quiet when a deer came out on the other side of the clearing and looked at us, and we looked at her, not moving, not even breathing, and she was the most beautiful thing I'd ever seen. Finally she turned and went back into the woods, without hurrying and we let our breath go and turned to smile at each other.

"April," he said abruptly. "Do you care if I write you from school? Or maybe call you up sometimes?"

My sixth sense was real! I tried not to dissolve too obviously into ecstasy. I said, "I'd like that."

"Good." He picked up my hand from the rock between us, looked at it with his head on one side. Then he leaned forward and gently kissed me. I held my breath as we stared at each other silently. Finally he said brusquely, "Well, pardner, let's push on and see if we can get to the trading post before dark."

"Before the wolves start prowling and the Apaches close in," I said. Nothing more personal was said. I don't think I could have stood it. In fact, though I loved every moment with him, I could hardly wait to be alone so I could *think* about it all.

When we got back to the house in the late afternoon, Brendan was there. I could see him sizing up Nick, blue eyes to blue, one boy so dark, one so fair, and both of them handsome. My mother appreciated that too, I could see it in her eyes. My father seemed quietly amused. When Nick had gone, and I started out with the dogs, Brendan walked a little way with me.

"He's too old for you, Ape," he said at once.

I sputtered. "Too old for *what*? What's to be too old about? He's just Jason's brother, that's all."

"Yeah? Where's Jason today?"

"He couldn't go."

"I figured."

"What does that mean?"

"Listen, the guy has to be seventeen anyway —"

"Sixteen and a half," I corrected him.

"And you're only fourteen —"

"Almost fifteen," I said icily.

He sighed. "Okay. But he's still too old for a sheltered kid like you. What'd he do, take you away from Little Brother?"

I was furious. "For your information, Brendan Snow, Jason has a girl, and Nick never took me away from him because we were just friends and associates in the first place."

"La-di-*dah*!" said Brendan, and grinned, and I forgave him. Partly.

"Anyway," I said, "Nick's going back to school tomorrow and so that's that."

"And not a minute too soon. I saw the way he looked at you, Ape. Or the way he tried not to look at you."

"I don't know what you're talking about."

"Yes, you do. I saw *you* trying not to look smug."

I took refuge in dignity. "The only thing Nicholas Barrett thinks about is the Navy. If I expected anything else I'd be a very disappointed *dope*. And I can understand him because I'm dedicated too. And now if you'll excuse me, I've got to give these dogs a run." And I took off.

I was a different person starting back to school. Not only had I Nick to think about, but I'd been seen with him — by Phyllis. She could never torment me again, I thought. I had to struggle to keep my mind on my work, but I managed somehow. After school we had a rehearsal — I was understudying the dancing daughter in *You Can't Take It with You* — and then, with the dogs, I was busy right until supper time. I was doing my homework that first night when Nick called, and I was nearly struck mute at the sound of his voice. I hadn't expected to hear from him so soon. He had only a few minutes, he said, but he wanted to say hello. I collected my wits and thanked him for the nice time on Saturday. "I keep thinking about that doe," I said.

"Me too," he answered, and that was it. Next time it was easier, and there was a "next time" every other night that week. By Sunday night we were having real conversations, and I astonished myself. My parents seemed so matter-of-fact about all this attention that I suspected them of overdoing it, but decided to let sleeping dogs lie.

Anyway, everything was wonderful those days. I wondered what Kathleen and Claire would say. Part of me wanted to write them all about him, the other part wanted to keep the whole precious thing to myself. I did talk a bit about him to my mother, both of us carefully behaving as if we knew it was just a casual friendship.

Two weeks later he came home for a weekend, and on Saturday we went horseback riding, again without Jason and Cindy, and the four of us went to the movies that night. Sunday morning he came around early to walk the dogs with me, and had breakfast at the house afterward. He had to return to school late that day, but we had time for a walk around town in the early afternoon. Anything that simple was a glorious adventure with Nick, but the most glorious moments were when he would hold me close to him and kiss me.

Twenty-eight

This was the way the next month went. He couldn't get home very often, but when he did we always did something special: another hike, riding again, going with Cindy and Jason to a dog show in Bixby, and supper afterward. When I think how I used to worry about dates! But even just walking the dogs was a celebration if Nick went along.

In between, he called, and sometimes he wrote. Mostly he talked about what was going on in school; anyone could have read these letters, but still they were private and I kept them to myself. One day he signed "Love," instead of "Be seeing you." I nearly wore that letter out in twenty-four hours.

He wasn't going to be home on my birthday, in fact I didn't expect to see him until the end of his school year, because they were all concentrating so hard on final exams. I wondered if he'd send me flowers for my birthday, or if his card would have a very significant personal message, and would I or wouldn't I show it to my parents? Decisions, decisions! But lovely ones.

We had a family party at the Snows on the Saturday nearest my birthday. The girls and

Brendan were all home for the weekend. Brendan hadn't brought his girl, though I wouldn't have minded now. It was the first time I'd seen him since he'd made the cracks about Nick. He was very much like himself while the family was together, but later when we four started out on the ritual hike to the brook, some local kids on horses stopped by to say hello to Claire and Kathleen, so Brendan and I were alone, and he became all at once very somber, and looked much older.

This made me uneasy. I put myself out to be nice and asked how Sue was. He looked off into space across the field and shrugged.

"I wouldn't know," he said. Obviously they'd broken up.

Because of my own happiness these days, I was extra-sorry for him and laid the condolences on a bit too thick, and he told me to shut up.

Three days later I'd just got in from school — my mother wasn't home and I was getting ready to dog-walk — when someone knocked on the back door and it was Nick. And there I was with a mouthful of peanut butter cookies and a milk mustache. He didn't seem to notice. He looked pretty tense.

"I've only got an hour," he said. "I got a chance to ride out with one of the teachers who had business here. Can we go to the park?"

"Sure," I said. "Just let me call my dog-people. And I ought to change."

"Don't," he said. "You look fine like that." My oldest jeans and much-darned sweater! Oh well, I'd like *him* in rags. I wiped my mouth and made my calls, saying I'd pick the dogs up later, and we set off for the park. Of course I was overjoyed to see him; I thought he looked strained because he could have only an hour with me.

The park was full of sunshine that day and the scent of the hyacinths they'd set out around the statues. The trees were all in fresh young leaves that rustled in the warm breeze. Birds sang and little kids raced around on their tricycles or pushed doll carriages. We took a path that led to a quieter place where we met very few people walking under the trees. When we came to the old granite horse trough Nick stopped me and said, "This is for you."

It was an old-fashioned gold locket on a chain; the locket had a beautifully carved dragon on it, and the dragon had a tiny green sparkling stone for an eye. I had the feeling of tears in my throat for the beauty of this moment, this day, the two of us alone under the trees as we'd been on the frozen lake the very first night. I opened the locket and it was empty.'

"It should have you in it," I said.

"*No.*" The word was half-strangled as if there were something in his throat too. I was frightened, not knowing why. I talked fast.

"This is my real birthday. It's the best one

of my life so far. This is the real celebration, today, with you."

"Maybe it won't be." He was pale. "I'm sorry, April!" Suddenly he took both my hands, holding them hard. His face looked the way mine feels when I'm trying not to cry. I remember thinking desperately, *how blue his eyes are!*

"We have to call it off, April," he said.

"What?" We hadn't planned anything; this visit had been a complete surprise.

"This. *Us.* I never counted on anything like it, April. All my life I've had one goal. The Navy, one way or another. I wouldn't let myself think of anything else." His hands squeezed even tighter, crushing my fingers around the locket and chain. "There'd be no girls, no time for girls, until I was where I wanted to be." His voice grew husky. "I never counted on you. You were just supposed to be the girl who was nice to my kid brother. A kid yourself. But April —"

"Don't, Nick," I pleaded. "Please don't! No more. Let's walk along and pretend you never said anything."

But he wouldn't let me move on.

"You're not just a nice kid. You're beautiful. I can't stop thinking about you. It's driving me up the wall, April. My work's beginning to suffer. Can't you *see*? My whole life's going out of whack. And I'm scared, April. I can't let it happen."

"Nick —" I could barely get his name out,

I was shivering so. "Why is it so awful? I think about you too, all the time." I tried to laugh.

He said fiercely, "You're an obsession with me. And you're only fifteen, and I've got to make Annapolis. Can't you see, April, if we go any farther we maybe can't stop, and that'll wreck us *both*?"

He was sweating, beginning to stammer. "I — I can't see anything else but your face — I can't get it out of my mind. Your hair — your eyes — you're the most beautiful thing I ever saw or ever will see."

I couldn't think of anything except to want to run, or to cover my ears. It was happening again, and I couldn't endure it. I wrenched my hands free, and put my arms around him and hugged him with all my might. "Please, Nick," I begged him. "Please don't do this to us!" I started to cry.

With a groan he wrapped his arms around me, and for the last time we embraced and kissed. It was so hard it hurt my mouth, and I remember thinking that if the hurt lasted I'd have that much of him, anyway.

We held on as if we could never let go. And then some people came strolling, and suddenly we were standing apart, resentful and heartbroken and out of breath, and there was a glisten in his eyes.

"I guess I'll go home," I said. "Alone."

"April," he said in a defeated voice. I waited a moment, but that was all. I turned away. The locket was still clutched in my hand. If only he'd said, "Wait till you're older." Or, "Wait till I get that appointment."

But no. He wanted no more of me. He couldn't ever be happy or comfortable with me the way I'd been with him. My looks had done it again. An obsession, he called me, and he already had one — the Navy. And that was the one he treasured the most.

Half-stunned I walked the long way home with the memory of his arms around me so hard and tight, and his mouth on mine. When I got there the last sting had gone from my lips, and I thought with a burst of agony, I haven't even got that now!

At least while I was alone in the house and then walking the dogs I had a chance to get over the first shock without having to think about my face. And that night I put on the performance of my life, appearing perfectly normal until I could go to bed. Luckily I had a lot of homework. But once in bed I sat holding the empty locket against my cheek and crying.

I hid it away for a long time, and months later I cut Jones out of a good clear snapshot, and put him in it.

They say your heart doesn't break if you're in love at fifteen, but look at Juliet. She was only fourteen. I'd been that age when I first met Nick, and now I was fifteen, and the thought of him was an ache in my throat day and night. I had to hide it, which was probably a good thing, though I don't know how much I fooled my parents.

The songs and poetry that I used to love for their romantic sadness I couldn't stand anymore. I went through my work in a trance, doing it well out of habit. Whenever I saw Jason it was a fresh wound, and he knew something was wrong, and he was hurt and puzzled, because he'd been so happy for us. I couldn't ignore him at Thespian meetings and rehearsals, and I could feel his anxiety even without looking at him.

One day he caught me unawares and blurted out, "Did you have a fight? Because maybe I could h-help." He was scarlet.

"No fight," I said. "We just decided it was best." How could I tell him that the truth was the same old cruelty? Being beautiful had cost me Nick.

I never looked in a mirror now except to check for neatness.

And this misery I couldn't tell Brendan. I could only numbly endure, hoping it would wear off. Then I'd hear a certain song or see someone in the distance that made me think of Nick, and the whole thing would be new and terrible.

By some freak of fate the girl who had the part of the dancing daughter in the play sprained her ankle and I got the part. I felt cheated because I should have been so happy and I couldn't be. But I did well. I really put everything into it, and afterwards I took a gloomy pride in my professionalism. Little did people guess what was really in my heart and soul, I thought.

I was sure that no one around me (certainly nobody in the whole high school) had loved and lost someone like Nicholas Barrett. If he thought *I* was beautiful — well, he was my golden Nicholas, and never, never, in my whole life would I get over losing him.

Twenty-nine

This year vacation glared before me like Death Valley under a noon sky in July. Somehow I had to cross it on foot, without water.

I had plenty to do, and we were going to Maine again, but the ache of loss was still strong with me. Once I saw Nick across the square downtown, and it almost turned me into stone. I couldn't move for a moment, and yet I knew I had to escape. It was like one of those dreams when you can't move your legs. Not like the first lovely dream when we flew over the ice.

Matt astonished everybody by announcing that he was going to a camp in Alaska for the summer. He came to the house one day to tell me about it, because he wouldn't be able to walk the dogs while I was away. He'd been saving for this adventure ever since he was big enough to shovel snow and mow lawns.

He was never loud and excitable, but now there seemed to be a light blazing away inside him, shining from his dark eyes, putting a warm burnish on his voice. "I'll be living in the wilds. Backpacking, riding horses. Meeting Indians and Eskimos. And" — now the

159

inner light really transformed his face — "I'll be working on a dig that dates from the time there was a land bridge across the Bering Sea."

All I could say was, "Oh, Matt!" I envied him so much for being able to go so far away that it hurt.

"Do they allow girls?"

"No!" He was as nearly horrified as I'd ever seen him. I managed a laugh.

"Send me a postcard."

"Sure."

With his usual forethought he'd been training a replacement all spring. This made me realize I'd better do the same. There'd always been little kids in the neighborhood who wanted to walk dogs with me, so I picked out Ginnie Marriot, who was twelve and like myself at that age in her feeling for animals.

I gave her a dollar fifty a week while I was training her. For the three weeks I was away she would get all the pay.

When Matt was gone, I missed him. That was funny, because I'd never seen that much of him.

I envied Matt. Everybody was doing something great; *meaningful* was the new word. But what was *I*? I was cheerful with the dogs because I couldn't take any meanness out on them, and I was a sunbeam around the house so my parents wouldn't guess how moody I really was. I didn't grandmother-sit any more because Mrs. Chisholm's other grand-daughter had moved back into town. I wouldn't be able to join a candy-striper class at the hospital until they started up in the fall, and I wasn't keen on that. One of Phyllis's things was running around in a pink dress and striped pinafore, shedding sweetness and light on defenseless patients.

Then one night my parents had a dinner party for some friends, and Mr. Lindquist, on whom I used to have a crush when I was little, asked me if I'd like a summer job with him. I'd be running errands to the post office and courthouse and other offices, and being a general help.

His wife laughed and said, "This is his way of redecorating the office."

"Think it over, April," Mr. Lindquist said. "All right with you, Tom?"

"She won't have to think it over, Walter," my father said. "I hadn't told her yet, but I've planned to take her into my office for the summer. She can make herself useful, and go home in mid-afternoon to look after her own clients." He smiled at my astonished face. "I was going to surprise you with it."

Mr. Lindquist beamed at me. "I'm disappointed. I'd love to have you in my office and so would my partners. But I know you'll be happy working with your father."

"Thank you," I said, flustered but not at all fooled. If my father had been planning it, it was only since Mr. Lindquist made his suggestion. And I knew at once that those two much younger partners loomed menacingly in my father's mind.

Never mind. I felt better than I'd been in weeks. Not exactly happy, but cheered up.

I got up early for the morning walks, and then by nine I was on my way downtown with my father. I tended the office when Miss Travis was out, and sometimes they were both out, and it was all mine. I learned filing. I went on errands, and I loved the importance of going to the courthouse. In addition to dusting the law library I was given a chance to do some research in it, and I assimilated eagerly everything Miss Travis explained to me.

Then in mid-afternoon I walked home and changed into shorts to take care of the dogs, with my apprentice Ginnie.

The job was really super, and my father seemed to enjoy my being in the office. Especially, I'm sure, when he thought of those very young partners of Mr. Lindquist's.

One day when both he and Miss Travis were out, the visiting son of a client came by to pick up some papers for his father. He had long fluffy sideburns, dark glasses, and California-type clothes. I'll never forget the expression on my father's face when he walked in and heard this colorful character inviting me to take a ride that evening in his Maserati.

"I'd love to," I said demurely, "but I have to walk a few dogs."

He laughed. "That's the most unique brush-off I've ever had."

I'm sure he thought I made it up. Two things about it made my day; my father's expression, and the fact that I hadn't done too badly with this sophisticated older man. I hadn't said much, but apparently I'd been, shall we say, *interesting*?

I hadn't really wanted to ride in his Maserati. Being interesting right out in the open was one thing, but how did you go on with it when they parked somewhere a long distance from houses and said, "Let's get acquainted"?

So I was satisfied on all counts, and Daddy could feel he'd saved his ewe lamb again.

Thirty

Brendan wasn't at the Labor Day gathering of the clan. He was visiting out of state somewhere. Sue wasn't mentioned, neither was any other girl, and Claire and Kathleen would have told me if there'd been one. They still liked Sue and I pulled a proper long face when they were sad about her. Little did they realize that I knew exactly what a break-up was like.

Now it was the eleventh grade, and Phyllis was back from camp, whizzing around town on the back of Bobby Saxon's new motorcycle. Matt was home from Alaska. He seemed bigger all over. His face was broader, stronger, and heavily tanned. What I'd scornfully called "moseying" was now seen as an unhurried but purposeful tempo.

Jason was still Old Short 'n' Shaggy, but with a difference. He'd learned enough from his job at the Civic Theatre's summer season to make some authoritative contributions to Thespian discussions, and he sounded very sure of himself. One thing, he'd no longer be a gopher. What were ninth and tenth graders for?

Mr. Hamilton had retired in June and our new sponsor was a Miss Kimball, fresh from directing college drama in New York. She was young, unconventional in her clothes, energetic, and full of ideas which sounded like fun. I was looking forward to a real part this year. In Thespians the first two years were like an apprenticeship. By the eleventh grade you were supposed to have more responsibility, either in parts or in some aspect of production.

I still had hopes of leaving at the end of the year, and planned my program accordingly. The guidance counselor asked me how my parents felt, and I said they were against it but I hoped to change their minds.

The pain had dulled down so I could enjoy poetry again, with a difference; now it was all personal. I memorized acres of Emily Dickinson and Elizabeth Barrett Browning. I even wrote some poems, apart from what we had to do for English.

My personal poetry was never seen by anyone else but me. What a waste, I thought with many a solemnn sigh. I toyed with the idea of sending an especially good sonnet to Nick, anonymously, but I couldn't do it. He had to be free of me. An obsession, he'd said . . . I took no satisfaction from that. I was too afraid for my future.

A widowed friend of my mother had a black Scottie pup, Clementina, who was one of my part-time clients. Occasionally Mrs.

Clark had to be away from home for a day, and then I would give Clementina her noon meal; they lived quite near the high school, so it was easy. I would have my sandwich and milk while she ate and then raced around the yard on her short legs.

One day when I had a free study period right after lunch, which meant I could study at home or anywhere else for that hour, I finished up a theme in the Clark kitchen and then took Clementina for a walk. It was a mild noon, more like April than November. We went in zig-zags from hydrant to tree to gate to hedge to tricycle to small kids to big dog, and so on all around the block. On the last lap I introduced a little leash training. We went up the brick walk with me looking down at Clementina and talking to her to keep her beside me without pulling. Suddenly she lunged forward with a juvenile roar and the leash went out of my hand.

A strange man was sitting on Mrs. Clark's front steps amid a weird assortment of luggage. He laughed at Clementina and put down his fist for her to smell, and she wagged all over as Scotties do, and became fascinated by his shoes.

He was a skinny man about my father's age, with longish hair, and he wore ordinary slacks, and a tweed jacket over a turtleneck sweater. He had a nice bony face with a big nose, and I saw twinkling blue eyes when he pushed his hair back from them. He looked at me for a moment and then said, "Byron said it best. 'And both were young, and one was beautiful.' "

"That must be Clementina," I said.

"Have it your way. I know who you are because my sister's told me about you. I'm Joe Winship. I knew your father and mother in high school, and I'm Olivia Clark's brother. Does that make me Clementina's uncle?"

"*She* thinks so." Clementina was prancing as well as a Scottie can prance.

His sister was expecting him, he said, but he'd arrive a day early. I showed him where the back door key was kept, and carried in his easel and paintbox while he took his other luggage. Clementina was in raptures.

"You painted the picture over the living room mantel," I said. "The one that's so hard to understand. I've tried to."

He smiled. "Don't. It can mean whatever you please."

"Well, good," I said. "I'll leave you with Clementina now. Don't let her out loose."

"I'm trustworthy even if I don't look it."

And so I left him and went back to school.

I came home from the library one Saturday afternoon, and there he was having coffee and cake in the kitchen with my parents. They were all laughing and having a great time. I was bad-tempered because Phyllis and Bobby had just roared by me, making me jump, and I knew darn well that what Phyllis had yelled at me hadn't been a friendly greeting.

167

Bobby went to everything Phyllis was in, and she went to all his games. Having him as a steady made her more arrogant than ever. And of course she was one up on me again, even if she didn't know it. She could have her Bobby. I could have no one, for the very same reason that turned her into my life-long enemy in the third grade.

I joined the party in the kitchen, eating cake and thinking grimly that everybody else had had a heck of a better time in high school than I was having.

Then my father said, "Mr. Winship wants to paint your portrait."

"Why?"

"That doesn't sound very polite," said my mother.

"Because I want to try my hand at portraits," Mr. Winship said seriously. "I'll be getting my sister to sit for me, and anyone else who has a face that appeals to me for one reason or another. The oil man now — he's a gem. And you know old Mrs. Chisholm? What a map of years *her* face is."

"You can't say mine's that interesting," I said.

"It is because it's young. The contrast, you see."

"Is that all?" I asked suspiciously.

"I won't lie to you. You must know you have a special kind of beauty. It's not like Mrs. Chisholm's, or even the oil man's, which is like a wild rocky shore. Right now yours is the beauty of a flower, a sapling, a young animal —"

"Which is what I am," I said reasonably. "All right, when do you want to begin?"

Thirty-one

We began two days after Christmas. I didn't spend the usual week with the Snows because the girls were going to Quebec on a school trip to ski and use their French. At home I worked on an assigned theme, and practiced on my new typewriter. I sat for Mr. Winship for two hours every morning; he liked that light best.

We decided I should wear a soft green shirt, open at the throat, but I could be comfortable in jeans because it would be a head-and-shoulders pose. I sat at a table with my arms folded on it.

Watching an artist at work was a new experience and I greedily absorbed everything as if I'd been dropped down in an exotic foreign country and had to catalogue every sight and sound and scent. He whistled softly to himself, sang under his breath, made comments that didn't call for answers. He told me at the first session that I held the pose like an expert. Philip Latimer had said something like that.

On the breaks we went down to the kitchen where his sister had coffee for him, and milk and cake for me, and I would play with

Clementina. But I was always glad to get back to work again. I felt important, and professional myself.

He told me about places he'd been, describing them so I wouldn't want to miss a word. He had funny or sad anecdotes about people he had met. I thought he lived a wonderful life, wandering with his paintbox wherever he chose. He'd struck out into the world direct from high school, and hadn't gotten his formal art education until he'd had some freedom first. He told me about all the jobs he'd taken; he'd do anything that would buy his meals and his paints. He'd finally won a scholarship, but after his schooling he'd taken to the road again.

In comparison with his life, my future looked like prison to me. The prospect of so many more years of school before I could be on my own filled me with despair. And *then* would I be on my own? A partner in a law firm, yes, but my father's firm, and I'd still be the little girl. I could have my own apartment downtown, but to others I'd still be April, resented and suspected.

"What does that expression mean?" Mr. Winship asked suddenly.

"What expression?" I was on guard.

"Now *that* look I know. Wary. Suspicious. I saw it the day your mother told you I wanted to paint you. *Why?* you asked. Tell me why you asked why."

"I know I'm beautiful!" I burst forth. "And I hate it! It's been nothing but trouble my whole life and I can't see anything but trouble ahead! People either get sloppy or they hate me. I thought you'd be sloppy. But when you explained, then it was all right. I mean, you made sense."

"It's the first time anybody ever told me that," he said. "Thank you." He went on painting. "How has it been a trouble to you? Your parents certainly don't exploit it. They haven't tried to make you into a movie star or a model."

"No. They've been great. A man did want to make me a model once." I told him about Philip Latimer.

"Did you want to do it?"

"Gosh, no! All the other kids thought I was nuts."

"Tell me about the other kids. Your friends." He sounded preoccupied; it made it easier for me to talk.

"I haven't any friends. I think I have, and then something happens." I tried to keep self-pity out of my tone. "It's not something I *do*. It's the way I look. Back in the third grade —"

So he got my autobiography. I did a good job if I do say so. I surprised myself by my objectivity. It would have been a fine summation to a jury, free of any disgusting sentimentality.

He put down his brush, sat back on his tall stool, and took out his pipe. "April, it's a sad story." He didn't say it humorously, and at once my poise was ruined. My eyes filled and I had to blow my nose.

172

"And the boys call me Ice Maiden and a cold fish and things like that!" I ran out of tissues and he brought me a whole roll of paper towels, which for some reason made me laugh.

"Forget it," I hiccupped. "I shouldn't have said anything. Brendan would tell me I'm a pain in the neck. You can say so too." I blew my nose on a paper towel.

"No. I think you need to talk. It's too bad about the girls, but as you grow older you'll meet other girls who are so sure of themselves they'll meet you on your own terms. But you have to know yourself what those terms are."

He lit his pipe, giving me a chance to clear my head. When he had the pipe going, he said, "You're a beautiful young girl, soon to become a beautiful woman. Most young things are beautiful in their newness and innocence. But it's what's inside the grown woman's head and heart that will constitute *her* beauty. The outside perfection doesn't mean a thing, except superficially. Do you follow?"

"Yes. Handsome is as Handsome does. I was brought up on it."

"It's a good way to live. Unfortunately a lot of other people stop at the face and never mind what's behind it. You'll have to come to terms with your own beauty before you can expect anyone else to." He walked around the studio puffing on his pipe. "April, when the boys call you the Ice Maiden they're tell-

173

ing you that they're afraid of you. You're sur-rounded by boys who in many ways are much younger than you, and they're in awe of you. Believe me, even grown men can feel threatened by such beauty."

"*Why?*" I was incredulous. "I'm just *me*. An ordinary person!"

He smiled. "Hardly ordinary, April. You must admit that. And these boys see you as something rare and fine — a living work of art — they don't know how to approach you! They're afraid of being snubbed, or laughed at, or *ignored*, which is even worse."

"But I've felt like that lots of times. And *boys* have done it to me."

"They armor themselves against you. Against the threat."

"*Nick.*" I'd said the name. Quietly, but it echoed in my head.

"Who's Nick?" he asked me, so I told him, and I didn't cry. What I felt was too much for tears.

When I finished he said quietly, "You'll thank him some day for being afraid. He knew you were both too young to handle what you felt, and both lives could have been scarred."

"Mine's scarred now!" I cried.

"Not permanently, April, believe me. Now there's another type of male," he went on, "who doesn't want any competition with his own charm and beauty. He wants to be the star, not reflect somebody else's glory. So you're a threat to *him* on that score."

"Did *you* ever feel threatened?" I asked him. "For any reason?"

"Inadequate is a better word for what I felt. I knew this girl in art school. She was so gorgeous and I was so proud to be seen with her. But I hadn't the courage to touch her. And years later I realized, looking back, that she'd really liked me, and gave me all sorts of chances."

"But what's anyone supposed to do?" I asked. "I mean, a girl just can't *tell* somebody she likes him. Either he'll run like a rabbit, or he'll think she's easy, and — you know."

"What I'm saying," he said patiently, "is that you are *you*, whole, complete in yourself, and you don't have to go through life simply reacting to what other people do. Don't worry about them as long as you know you're right. What these kids think of you comes from their own fears and worries — you're all walking tightropes, you know." He knocked out his pipe in an ashtray and went back to the easel. I took the pose.

"So don't be impatient. Don't do anything crazy out of desperation. What these kids think of you, and whether or not any little boy asks you out, isn't going to matter much a year or so from now. If you're secure in yourself, without any doubts of your own worth as a person, eventually you'll have good friends, men and women both. People who'll see past the face. They'll *like* you, April, and that's important."

I listened, nodding. But what he said seemed to have no meaning for me except to underline the fact that behind my face I was a prisoner in solitary confinement, and would be — for how long?

Thirty-two

I looked forward to the sittings, even though we never talked like that again, because I believed Mr. Winship was the one person in the world who knew the truth about me. Brendan might have sensed it, but he'd be like my parents, acting as if I were just any normal kid. They *had* to be that way.

After the blinding glare of enlightenment had dimmed a little, I thought, *All right, I'm different and I accept it. Instead of seeing my looks as a handicap, I'll use them as an asset. Wouldn't that be coming to terms with myself?*

Naturally I didn't introduce the subject at the dinner table, and I didn't tell Mr. Winship either. I had a feeling he'd tell me that wasn't quite what he'd meant.

But now that I'd made up my mind, I felt better. I dreamed myself onto posters and talk shows. I modeled expensive cosmetics and priceless jewelry in magazines, and thousand-dollar outfits in Paris or Rio de Janeiro. I saw mothers biting their lips and otherwise expressing chagrin while I gleamed enigmatically green-eyed at them from magazine racks.

Phyllis, away at college, would be half-strangled with fury when her roommate tossed down a high-fashion magazine and said, "Isn't April Adams simply *superb*?"

Occasionally I'd have lunch with Matt when he came back from a dig in Asia, or with Jason who'd be a producer of a Broadway hit — I might as well dream big for them too. Pam, having become a great actress, would be glad to invite me backstage after a performance. Not that I wouldn't know a lot of theatrical people already. I'd probably have offers myself.

It was a nice way to go to sleep at night.

Some of us took our college board exams now, and I wasn't worried while waiting for results. I knew I'd done well. Besides, I had my new career to think of. I would entertain Claire and Kathleen in my spacious apartment in New York. Brendan would still be in medical school when I had already become a sensation, but when I could get away I might fly unexpectedly to Vermont and make a big fuss over him. The other students would be properly impressed by his glamorous cousin.

People would say about me, "She's mysterious. She will never belong to any man. There was one, once . . ."

Ah, Nick. On the bridge, at sea, would he dream of me? Would we meet years later, he as a handsome admiral and I as a woman of the world? I sighed, and returned to problem *a*: How to convince my parents I should graduate this year. After that came problem *b*: What was the best way to tell them about my modeling career? And *c*: How best to use the time until I was legally of age and could start said career?

However, *b* and *c* could be put off until I had dealt with *a*. And it was easier to leap over all intervening difficulties and see myself established as the darling of the studios and the toast of New York. This last phrase I particularly fancied.

I went happily to the first meeting of Thespians after the break for holidays and exams. At this meeting we expected to discuss our big spring production, as we'd done with Mr. Hamilton. There'd be arguments during several meetings until the list of plays was boiled down to a very few. Then we'd vote for the final choice. Some of the Intellectuals always pushed for Shaw, Ibsen, O'Casey, or O'Neill. Others wanted more modern works.

This year we found out that Miss Kimball was a new broom indeed. She told *us* what the play would be. *The Merchant of Venice.* She shone with an arrogant confidence. "I always swore I could turn a high school drama group into a Shakespeare company. This group has more than enough talent to carry it off!"

Her fervor was catching, you could see the little fires starting up here and there.

"But why that one?" asked a blond senior girl. "Why not *Romeo and Juliet?* Or *Hamlet?*"

Jason whispered to me, "She sees herself as Juliet or Ophelia."

"If you don't have the right Shylock the whole thing is a bust," a boy argued, and I thought of Reid Bennett, now lost in business administration.

"Don't worry! This play is my favorite. I *know* I can give it my best." Miss Kimball's voice rang out. "Now I'll want some really *vibrant* ideas on color schemes, settings, lights, and music. I'll expect volunteers for those committees to check in with me after school tomorrow. We'll also have try-outs for the following." She read a list of characters. One was Portia, and I'd have sat up straight even if Jason hadn't poked me.

"Over to you, Portia," he muttered.

That night Portia dominated my dreams; she was mine as she always had been. The modeling career went to the back of the closet, at least for now. I was wholly involved and dedicated. During school the next day several kids asked if I was trying out, and my English teacher wished me luck. Even Matt, meeting me in the library, emerged from his fog of thought to say, "I hear you're doing Portia."

"Trying out," I corrected. "There'll be others." But not many, I was sure.

"You shouldn't have any trouble," Matt said gruffly.

I was glad I had no friend to go with me for moral support. I wanted to sit alone at one side while I waited. I tried to concentrate on the other readings but all the time I seemed to be quivering inside. When Miss Kimball called "Portia," I leaped up as if that were really my name.

There were only three of us trying out for the part, which convinced me that most of the girls in the club felt the part was mine.

There was the conversation with Nerissa in Scene II, and then, of course, the "quality of mercy" speech. The first girl to read, with Miss Kimball as Nerissa, had trouble with her breathing, went too fast, and fell all over the words. I took a lesson from that; Miss Kimball wasn't going to intimidate *me*.

She didn't. I'd read the part aloud too often. I was Portia, Portia was me, and Miss Kimball wasn't a teacher, she was my maid Nerissa. There was even some applause from the darkened auditorium when we finished that scene.

Then on to the diamond, the courtroom scene, and the beautiful words that I wanted so passionately to make Shylock understand and believe, so that his heart would be moved.

This time when we finished the applause was more than scattered. It was hearty, and lasted until Miss Kimball held up her hand.

"We're busy here," she said curtly. "Thank you, April." I went back to my seat, passing the third candidate on the way. She gave me a tight little grin. It was Katie Hardin, the blond girl who'd spoken up yesterday.

She was nervous in the part, probably

from seeing herself so long as Juliet or Ophelia. Portia is far different in her humor and wit and determination.

I clapped for her when she finished, and sat back to wait for the final word. Mr. Hamilton always had a committee, which was part of their training, but Miss Kimball had made herself the sole judge.

At last she called us together at the front of the auditorium, below the stage. Those left in the seats would be trying out tomorrow, or maybe go into some other part of production. There were also some non-Thespians who'd come alone with their friends, or just to listen in; the auditorium wasn't off-limits. They talked quietly among themselves as the candidates collected around Miss Kimball.

She gave out the parts without any hesitation. It hadn't taken her long to make up her mind. Mercifully she took the girls first, creating a radiant Nerissa, a delighted Jessica.

And Katie Hardin was Portia.

It was like Phyllis becoming Princess, only much worse, because this time I'd been so absolutely sure. Everybody was surprised, even Katie. Throats were cleared, somebody touched my arm. I stood rigid.

Miss Kimball rustled papers. "Now for Antonio," she began. She glanced at me.

"What *is* the matter, April? What are you staring at?"

"Why didn't I get the part?" I blurted out.

"You have no right to ask that," she said. "The decision has been made."

"Miss Kimball," Katie began timidly.

"You're Portia, Katie. You'd better go start learning your first scene. Now for Antonio —"

Katie went fast up the nearest aisle. I said, "Miss Kimball, Portia should be mine. She's always been mine. Everybody knows that. Didn't you hear them clap?"

"If you brought your fan club with you, that's no concern of mine."

"I didn't bring anyone with me!" I cried. "If they clapped it was because I was the best. You *know* I was the best!"

"I know nothing of the kind," she said coldly. She put her papers down on the piano and gave me her full attention. "I do know that you're a spoiled little girl who's probably been manipulating teachers from the first day at kindergarten. I've had my eye on you ever since I came to this school. I know all about girls like you. You've grown up thinking you have a right to anything you want, simply because of some freak of nature you're better looking than most. Well, you may have had this school in your pocket up till now, but beauty doesn't prejudice *me*, young woman."

She swung around to pick up her papers. I was trembling. "Yes, it does!" I said. "Because you just turned me down on account of it. You must have hated me because of it from the first time you saw me. And if that isn't prejudice, what is?"

I marched up the aisle, knowing that in a moment I'd be crying and I had to get out quick. And once I was out of the building I'd never come back into it.

Thirty-three

From the seats I was passing a familiar laugh pealed out, and Phyllis's voice mocked me. " 'April, April, laugh thy girlish laughter; then, the moment after, weep thy girlish tears.' "

I stopped, blinded but with my fists clenched.

"Hi, April," someone said at my other side. "Come on." It was New Boy Matt.

Without speaking we walked straight up the aisle, out into the corridor, and across to the front doors. On the way he gave me a handkerchief. Clean. "I haven't got my books and my coat," I said thickly.

"Where are they?"

I told him, with difficulty, where I'd been sitting in the auditorium. "I'll get them. Don't you go anywhere." I mopped my streaming eyes with one half the handkerchief and my nose with the other half, and the flood went on and on. Matt came back with my things.

"Fix your scarf and put on your cap before we go out, it's cold," he said. I obeyed soddenly. "Want to take a walk?"

"I don't care," I said. "I can't go home

looking like this, because I have to tell them something."

"What?" he asked, chivalrously holding the door for me.

"I'm out of Thespians and I'm out of school. I'll never go back after that. You heard her, didn't you?"

"Who could miss it? She raised her voice on purpose. Couldn't miss the other one, either. The cry of the Mottled Crazybird."

Fantastic! Matt had taken charge. Matt was trying to make me laugh. I wanted to give him a closer look, but I was too stunned by Miss Kimball's massive unfairness to see anything else clearly.

We walked on a quiet street under bare trees. "What do you mean, you aren't going back to school?"

"Just that. I can finish up by correspondence course from somewhere. . . . I wanted to graduate this June anyway, and I've already got enough points to leave right now." I stopped in the middle of the sidewalk. "Matt, that part was mine! And look why she gave it away! Because of no reason at all!"

"Oh, she had her reason, she told you. It's a kind of sick reason, but it's real enough. . . . Why give it to her?" He spoke as slowly and quietly as ever but, being thankful for his sudden appearance and his handkerchief, I was bound to listen. "If you don't show up again, she'll convince a lot of people she was telling the truth."

"What do I care about that bunch?"

"What about the kids who never thought it before about you? I always heard The Thespians were a pretty good bunch."

"They are," I admitted.

"Seems to me," he went on in his moderate way, "you could really get her where it hurts by sticking around and being a ray of sunshine. What could you do if you didn't act?"

"Work on costumes," I said doubtfully.

"Come on, it's too cold to stand still." We walked.

"What if I — not that I'm going to do it — but just supposing I tried to get into Wardrobe, and she turned me down for that?"

"Don't try," he said reasonably. "Wait till the kids get to work, then ask *them* if you can help. After all, it's for the school, not for her."

"Well," I said grumpily. We stopped to cross, and had to wait while a motorcycle charged down the block. At the sight of Bobby Saxon, zippered, helmeted, and gauntleted, but with his grin showing, I groaned. He had Phyllis behind him.

"Look *happy*," Matt said in my ear. I waved and yelled "Hi!" Phyllis's smile vanished, not Bobby's.

We stopped again at the corner of my street. "Well, thanks, Matt," I said, feeling inarticulate.

"For what? I just moseyed along." He gave me that rare but merry grin. "Hey, was I dreaming or did I actually hear Phyllis spouting *poetry*?"

"My gosh!" I said. "She did! William Watson. We read it in the seventh grade. She's probably been waiting all this time for a chance to use it on me."

"Shows you're good for something, doesn't it?" he said solemnly. He flapped one hand. "So long. See you tomorrow, if you haven't left town." Before he walked away we looked at each other for a long moment — Matt looked somehow different to me.

My mother wasn't home, and I'd gotten rid of all signs of tears by the time I'd finished dog-duty. I told my parents I'd lost the part, and I didn't give them any more details.

"I'm going to work on costumes," I went quickly on. "It ought to be fun, all those colors, and loads of junk jewelry, and the boys having to wear tights." I gave a weak giggle.

I looked up Jason the next day and asked him who'd been put in charge of Wardrobe. He wanted to say something about what had happened, but I wouldn't let him.

"That was yesterday. I don't want to think about it anymore." The words were braver than I was, because I knew the first glimpse of Miss Kimball was going to bring back the familiar shame and hurt and anger. But you're growing up now, Ape, I told myself, so you know there's something wrong with *her*, not you.

The costume chairman was glad of another good needlewoman, and would let me know when the planning and buying was done and it was time to cut out, fit, and sew.

"When you walked out yesterday, nobody thought you'd ever be back."

I shrugged. "I care about Thespians, not about her."

"You should have the part. Katie's on Cloud Nine about it today, but maybe you'd better learn the whole thing in case she loses her courage."

"Hah! Miss Kimball would probably do it herself before she'd let me."

Not that it was easy to be a good sport. Against my will I listened in a few rehearsals and, even allowing for the fact that it was early yet, Katie was weak and childish. Nerissa and Jessica were better, but it didn't seem as if sparks could ever fly on that stage.

Katie thought she was going to do well. Miss Kimball had convinced her by sheer force of will, and was coaching her on the side. Shylock, after one rehearsal, dropped out. Not that he was much good anyway; he didn't have Reid Bennett's feeling for the character. Besides, he'd wanted to do something modern. The new Shylock was drafted, and behaved accordingly.

"It's a mess," I told Jason, who had brought his lunch to my table one noon. "We're all going to work so hard to stage it, and they'll be so awful."

Jason grinned. "Look, on the big night I'll find a way to break her leg so they'll have to use you, because Miss Kimball's too big to fit into Katie's costumes."

"Then she'd break Shylock's leg so she can

189

do him," I suggested. "Heck, I just wish I didn't care what happened."

After that afternoon when Matt had materialized like a good genie in the auditorium, he'd gone back to being New Boy Matt, but whenever we saw each other there was something new between us. Then he came along on his bike one day when I was out on the Cavendish road, as he'd done once when we were twelve.

"I got thinking," he said abruptly. "One good thing. Phyllis isn't in Thespians. She'd have tried out and probably got the part."

"Thank *you*," I said. "Gives me something to be grateful for."

"Another item." He walked his bike beside the dogs and me. "Just think how frustrated Miss Kimball's going to be on the Night, and how scared Katie's going to be, knowing you're the one who should be doing it and that everybody else knows it. So if the show's going to be rotten, and you can't help it, you might as well enjoy it. That's my motto."

He made me laugh. "Listen, Matt, I never heard a thing about what you did in Alaska last summer."

"I sent you a postcard, didn't I?"

"Yes, but that's nothing. I want to know what you dug up."

"I'll show you sometime. I've got some pictures too. But hey, I've got a dig of my own out on Orr's Hill." He had to stop walking to say it, and his eyes were very bright.

"No kidding! *Tell* me!"

"Well, it's on an old farm. Last fall I painted the house for the lady that lives there. It's not a working farm anymore, she just has chickens. I'd go roaming around on my lunch break, and I followed the brook where it goes downhill along this rocky course, and I came to the swamp, and I found an arrowhead in the pebbles where water flowed out of the swamp. I found some flint chips and a good scraper too. So I dug around the banks a bit and found some pieces of pottery."

"Oh, Matt! How old is it, do you think?"

"Pretty old," he said cautiously. "When I get a lot of stuff I'm going to take it to a man in Cavendish who's an expert."

"And she's letting you dig there, huh?"

"Yep, as long as it's just me, not a gang." He leaned down abruptly and scratched Lissa's back. His voice came up indistinctly. "I think you could come along sometime if you wanted to. Like this Saturday."

"How do we get there?" I asked.

"It's not far on bikes. We'll go if the thaw still hangs on. If it snows or freezes, the digging's no good, of course."

Thirty-four

The thaw held, and Saturday was soft and cloudy-bright. When I saw that it was a good day, I knew that to go poke around in a distant swamp for Indian relics was what I wanted to do most in the world. It was like going to another country, and that was what I needed after an emotionally exhausting week.

I gave all my dogs a good workout, then went to sit for Mr. Winship for an hour. I told him what I was planning, and he told me about painting among the Navahos, and some of their ceremonies; and in no time the hour was gone.

We met at ten at the corner of Main and Chestnut. (My mother had managed not to beam while she made suggestions for my lunch and contributed extra brownies.) We rode out of town on Chestnut toward Orr's Hill, then turned off the main road and climbed the hill by a narrow dirt lane, so steep in places that we had to walk our bikes. I discovered one didn't need to scintillate with Matt, he liked his own thoughts as well as anybody else's conversation, unless that was about archeology.

Crows shouted warnings about us from the pine woods and across empty pastures. We saw a fox out mousing. The pale sun came warmly through the thin clouds, and there was a dry ledge where we could put our food and extra jackets. There were chickadees and blue jays, and this pure lovely sense of distance from all that was crowded and mean.

Matt said vaguely, "Just poke around and show me anything that looks like anything."

"Great," I said. "Gives me a lot to choose from. There are so many anythings that look like anythings."

"Funny," he said, standing in the brook and groping with bare hands in the icy brown water for something stuck between the rocks. He brought it out and stood examining it from every angle. I dug in the soft damp sandy earth on the bank, very carefully as he'd warned me.

It was fun being there whether I found anything or not, but it was even better when Matt came up with a felsite knife in perfect condition. He couldn't keep from grinning every time he looked at it. I actually found a piece of pottery, and an almost-whole point.

"Okay, let's eat now," he said finally. We sat on the ledge and swapped sandwiches and dessert, content without much to say, listening to the birds, a distant train whistle, the old lady's dog barking up at the house.

We started back at two, because we both had work to do at home. Matt was methodical. All our finds, even the smallest chip, were each carefully wrapped and packed in his lunch box.

"What a nice day," I said. "Thank you for asking me."

"You can come again," he said. He raised one hand as if he was going to touch me, but he didn't.

Alternately walking and riding, we reached the foot of the lane and went out onto the main road. There was a fair amount of traffic, but it came in little bursts with long pauses between. We rode along at the side, Matt ahead.

Occasionally there was a motorcycle, once three big ones together. A tractor-trailer truck roaring by created enough draft to make me nervous, but after that there was a quiet spell.

Then another motorcycle came along. From the sound it was either smaller than the earlier ones, or else he was deliberately holding down his speed. Then a burst of power right behind me startled me into veering toward the shoulder, and the soft gravel made me wobble and almost tip down the slope toward the ditch.

"Sorry about that, April!" Bobby Saxon yelled over the noise. With a curious lack of surprise I watched him and Phyllis pass Matt, waving and yelling, and then they planed around the next bend.

Of course Phyllis would show up out here, I thought. Of course she'd have to appear in my good day. She's psychic. If I ever get married she'll probably pop up on the honeymoon and be the one to get carried over my threshold.

But she couldn't spoil today if I didn't let her. It was all up to me, and I should be completely immune to her by now. I shut her out of my mind and pedaled faster to catch up with Matt as we went around the curve.

And stopped.

The motorcycle had shot across the road, gone over a stone wall, and plunged down a steep field. Now it rested on its side against a big oak, still running. Bobby lay near it, like a helmeted, goggled, anonymous, horribly jointless dummy. Phyllis crouched beside him in a tight knot.

Without a word we swerved across the road and dismounted by the stone wall, and ran down through the field. I knew now what chaos was; it was my mind, in those first terrible moments.

Matt ran over to the cycle and shut it off. Then I heard Phyllis crying. Chaos ceased; I knelt beside her and put my arms around her shuddering shoulders. "He's dead, he's dead," she moaned.

I didn't want to look at Bobby. I remember thinking Phyllis didn't know it was me holding her because she still had on her helmet, and couldn't hear me, and she couldn't take her eyes off Bobby. Matt knelt and put his head down on Bobby's chest and listened.

"He's not dead," he said laconically. Bobby

wasn't bleeding from an artery either. But he *looked* lifeless, and the goggles and helmet made it worse.

"I'll get an ambulance," Matt said. "I may be a little while getting to a telephone if I can't flag down a car. So don't panic." He was talking to me. "And don't move or touch him. Oh, here." He unzipped his jacket and put it over Bobby's chest and shoulders. "It's not much, but it'll help." He looked intently into my face. "Will you be all right?"

"Yes," I said, knowing it had to be so. He went up the field, not moseying. I took off my jacket and put it over more of Bobby. Meanwhile Phyllis, still in this tight knot, rocked back and forth crying softly.

"Matt's gone for help," I said to her but she acted deaf. "Come on, take off that darned thing," I said, trying to find out how the helmet worked. She pushed my hands away and took it off herself. Her eyes kept filling and running over. She looked into my face and sobbed, "He's dead."

"No, he isn't, Phyllis," I said. "Matt says he isn't."

"I'll die too," she wept. I put my arms around her.

"No, no, Phyllis."

"I wanted him to go faster, to show off," she wailed. "I don't know what happened!" She didn't fight me, she clung and she was trembling with her terror. I found myself patting her back. It was weird, but mostly I was concerned with trying to give her some help. She wasn't Phyllis now so much as a shocked and frightened girl.

"He's probably just knocked out," I told her. "His helmet should take care of his head." But there wasn't much else I could say because he looked so awful. Bobby Saxon, that sturdy little boy kicking a soccer ball around; Bobby Saxon, high school star athlete and always with that happy grin for everybody. I couldn't make him be the thing on the ground.

Phyllis and I sat there, my arms around her while she cried without stopping. I thought how many times she'd seen me in tears or fighting them, and she'd enjoyed it. I thought how strange it all was, and meanwhile there was this consuming fear that if Bobby weren't already dead he might be dying while we sat there.

Then all at once everybody was coming down the slope. Everybody being ambulance attendants and Matt, and a couple of other men. Bobby was checked, cautiously moved onto a stretcher, wrapped in blankets, our jackets returned. They started the careful journey up the hill to the road.

Phyllis grabbed at my hand. "Come with me."

"We both can't go in the ambulance, Phyl," I said.

"You've got to come. I'm so scared. *Please*," she begged.

One of the other men said, "I'd be glad to run you both to the hospital." The second one had a pickup truck and he offered to bring along the motorcycle and our two bikes. Matt stayed with him. I felt like begging Matt as Phyllis had pleaded with me. As if he sensed my panic, he said, "I'll see you at the hospital." The ambulance had already taken off.

Phyllis and I sat in the front seat with the stranger, a rumpled fatherly sort who kept telling us it would be all right. Phyllis was slumped and silent now, but I could feel the vibrations of fear running through her.

At the hospital the man left us outside Emergency, still saying everything would be all right but that I should call our mothers.

Phyllis said loudly, "Not mine!"

"Thank you very much," I said to the man.

He nodded. "I'll call up by and by to see how the boy makes out."

I asked the nurse about Bobby, and all she could say was, "They're examining him now. . . . Is that *Phyllis*?"

I'd forgotten Phyllis worked here. She ignored the nurse's offer of hot tea and a mild sedative. I guided her to a seat, sat down with her and kept my arm around her shoulders. I thought about Bobby's parents. Should I call them? My stomach rebelled. But somebody ought to. Maybe Matt —? Where was he, anyhow? How long ago had we been peacefully eating on that warm ledge by the distant brook in another country?

I could call my mother and ask her to call

Bobby's. But when I tried to take my arm away, Phyllis wouldn't let me. "I'm so scared," she said abjectly. And the Emergency supervisor was busy bandaging somebody up, so I couldn't ask her to call.

"Why don't you want your mother?" I asked Phyllis.

"Because she'd make a scene," said Phyllis. "I just want to sit here and wait till — wait —" She choked. "If he's badly hurt, what'll I do? What if he's broken his back and he's paralyzed?"

"Don't think such things," I said.

"I love him," she said. "My mother doesn't think I'm old enough. If I told her I loved Bobby she'd have a fit." She turned those wet, red-rimmed, swollen eyes on me. "But *you* know how it is, don't you?"

"Sure, I know." Oh yes, I did. This was one thing we shared, though she'd never know how.

She was calmer now. "Thanks for staying with me," she said suddenly. "I was all alone in the world, and it was the most terrible feeling I'd ever had, and of all the people in the universe to show up, it was you." She said it wonderingly. "I never thought I'd be so happy to hear your voice."

"I never would have believed it either," I said.

She studied her hands. "I've always hated you, since the third grade."

"Why?" I asked bluntly. "Phyllis, I was crazy about you when you came into our room. I thought you were so — well, now I'd call it dynamic — and so *sophisticated*. The only thing I wanted in the world was to have you for a friend. A *best* friend."

Her face went blank with astonishment. "You're kidding."

"No! The reason I took the blame about the apples that day was so you'd think I was super. But you thought — well, we know what you thought."

"I thought you were the princess of the third grade and you were going to put the new kid in her place. I had a chip on my shoulder that was a whole log. We'd moved so often before we came here and I was always the new kid, and do you know what *that*'s like? When you can't help it?"

"No, but I know what it's like to be treated like a typhoid carrier when you can't help it. I guess you made a place for yourself all right, Phyllis." I wasn't mean about it. "You've been having a ball in school all these years."

"Not really," she said, "because you were always there. No matter what I did and said, I couldn't get rid of you."

"Well, Phyllis, you haven't exactly been *my* sunshine, my only sunshine. I'd wake up thinking, Phyllis Clements is out to get me!"

"And now look at us," she said. She was too worn out to be anything but quiet. Not knowing what was going on behind those closed doors was a great flattener. "When I came to, down in that field today — and it happened so *fast*, April, I can't get over that. I mean we seemed to fly over that wall and we couldn't do a thing about it — Anyway, suddenly I was all alone with Bobby, thinking he was dead, and we could have been on the *moon*. And then you were there. The way you always have been. And I was never so glad to see anybody in my life."

There was nothing to say. We sat side by side, my arm still around her. We were like that when Matt came in, looking serious but utterly competent.

"We took the motorcycle to the Saxons'. They're on the way now. Our bikes are outside, April."

"All right. I'll wait till the Saxons come, and —"

Phyllis clutched at my free hand. "Don't leave me with them! If it's bad news they'll be so upset and I won't know what to do!"

"I'll wait," I promised, wishing for my mother. But here we were, and there was nothing to do but go through with it.

"Then I'll wait too," said Matt and sat on the other side of me, his shoulder comfortably against mine. I was aware of his quiet assurance and support and leaned against him slightly.

The doctors had their report ready by the time the Saxons arrived; Bobby had some broken ribs and a slight concussion. He was out of sports for a time but his good humor remained. Phyllis wasn't humbled for long by her experience, but it wouldn't have seemed right for Phyllis ever to be meek. After all, what had attracted me to her in the first place?

We'd never be close chums but at least we weren't enemies. The only person I told about our conversation was Brendan, because he'd had to listen to all my hard-luck stories over the years and I wanted to show him I could say more than "It's not fair," or "It's not my fault."

He'd made up with Sue so I had to snatch time alone with him when I could. Still, I wished him happiness, I allowed myself to like Sue and found that she liked me. She saw behind my face, Matt did too. We put in some happy hours grubbing around in his dig, and as my reward for being a careful excavator and finding a Folsom point, I could go with him to visit the man in Cavendish who was an expert.

I decided the senior year might be a good idea after all. I'd like to enjoy at least some part of my high school experience, and now I was going to. If boys flocked — or didn't flock — what difference? Besides, there was Matt. More and more I looked forward to being with him.

I also decided that modeling would be a drag. By the time I'd put in another summer at my father's office, I knew that the law was my profession.

My portrait, to be titled simply "Spring," would appear in Mr. Winship's show next summer. I wondered if Nick would ever see it.

Oh! Our Shakespeare production wasn't very good. Some of the actors weren't up to their material. But the staging was neat, and the costumes were *smashing*.